Tatterdemalion by John Galsworthy

John Galsworthy was born at Kingston Upon Thames in Surrey, England, on August 14th 1867 to a wealthy and well established family. His schooling was at Harrow and New College, Oxford before training as a barrister and being called to the bar in 1890. However, Law was not attractive to him and he travelled abroad becoming great friends with the novelist Joseph Conrad, then a first mate on a sailing ship.

In 1895 Galsworthy began an affair with Ada Nemesis Pearson Cooper, the wife of his cousin Major Arthur Galsworthy. The affair was kept a secret for 10 years till she at last divorced and they married on 23rd September 1905.

Galsworthy first published in 1897 with a collection of short stories entitled "The Four Winds". For the next 7 years he published these and all works under his pen name John Sinjohn. It was only upon the death of his father and the publication of "The Island Pharisees" in 1904 that he published as John Galsworthy.

His first play, The Silver Box in 1906 was a success and was followed by "The Man of Property" later that same year and was the first in the Forsyte trilogy. Whilst today he is far more well know as a Nobel Prize winning novelist then he was considered a playwright dealing with social issues and the class system. Here we publish Villa Rubein, a very fine story that captures Galsworthy's unique narrative and take on life of the time.

He is now far better known for his novels, particularly The Forsyte Saga, his trilogy about the eponymous family of the same name. These books, as with many of his other works, deal with social class, upper-middle class lives in particular. Although always sympathetic to his characters, he reveals their insular, snobbish, and somewhat greedy attitudes and suffocating moral codes. He is now viewed as one of the first from the Edwardian era to challenge some of the ideals of society depicted in the literature of Victorian England.

In his writings he campaigns for a variety of causes, including prison reform, women's rights, animal welfare, and the opposition of censorship as well as a recurring theme of an unhappy marriage from the women's side. During World War I he worked in a hospital in France as an orderly after being passed over for military service.

He was appointed to the Order of Merit in 1929, after earlier turning down a knighthood, and awarded the Nobel Prize in 1932 though he was too ill to attend.

John Galsworthy died from a brain tumour at his London home, Grove Lodge, Hampstead on January 31st 1933. In accordance with his will he was cremated at Woking with his ashes then being scattered over the South Downs from an aeroplane.

Index of Contents

TATTERDEMALION

PART I

OF WAR-TIME

CHAPTER I

THE GREY ANGEL

Her predilection for things French came from childish recollections of school-days in Paris, and a hasty removal thence by her father during the revolution of '48, of later travels as a little maiden, by diligence, to Pau and the then undiscovered Pyrenees, to a Montpellier and a Nice as yet unspoiled. Unto her seventy-eighth year, her French accent had remained unruffled, her soul in love with French gloves and dresses; and her face had the pale, unwrinkled, slightly aquiline perfection of the 'French marquise' type—it may, perhaps, be doubted whether any French marquise ever looked the part so perfectly.

How it came about that she had settled down in a southern French town, in the summer of 1914, only her roving spirit knew. She had been a widow ten years, which she had passed in the quest of perfection; all her life she had been haunted by that instinct, half-smothered in ministering to her husband, children, and establishments in London and the country. Now, in loneliness, the intrinsic independence of her soul was able to assert itself, and from hotel to hotel she had wandered in England, Wales, Switzerland, France, till now she had found what seemingly arrested her. Was it the age of that oldest of Western cities, that little mother of Western civilisation, which captured her fancy? Or did a curious perversity turn her from more obvious abodes, or was she kept there by the charm of a certain church which she would enter every day to steep herself in mellow darkness, the scent of incense, the drone of incantations, and quiet communion with a God higher indeed than she had been brought up to, high-church though she had always been? She had a pretty little apartment, where for very little—the bulk of her small wealth was habitually at the service of others—she could manage with one maid and no "fuss." She had some "nice" French friends there, too. But more probably it was simply the war which kept her there, waiting, like so many other people, for it to be over before it seemed worth while to move and re-establish herself. The immensity and wickedness of this strange event held her, as it were, suspended, body and spirit, high up on the hill which had seen the ancient peoples, the Romans, Gauls, Saracens, and all, and still looked out towards the flat Camargue. Here in her three rooms, with a little kitchen, the maid Augustine, a parrot, and the Paris Daily Mail, she dwelt as it were marooned by a world event which seemed to stun her. Not that she worried, exactly. The notion of defeat or of real danger to her country and to France never entered her head. She only grieved quietly over the dreadful things that were being done, and every now and then would glow with admiration at the beautiful way the King and Queen were behaving. It was no good to "fuss," and one must make the best of things, just as the "dear little Queen" was doing; for each Queen in turn, and she had seen three reign in her time, was always that to her. Her ancestors had been uprooted from their lands, their house burned, and her pedigree diverted, in the Stuart wars—a reverence for royalty was fastened in her blood.

Quite early in the business she had begun to knit, moving her slim fingers not too fast, gazing at the grey wool through glasses, specially rimless and invisible, perched on the bridge of her firm, well-shaped nose, and now and then speaking to her parrot. The bird could say, "Scratch a poll, Poll," already, and "Hullo!" those keys to the English language. The maid Augustine, having completed some small duty, would often come and stand, her head on one side, gazing down with a sort of inquiring compassion in her wise, young, clear-brown eyes. It seemed to her who was straight and sturdy as a young tree both wonderful and sad that Madame should be seventy-seven, and so frail—Madame who had no lines in her face and such beautiful grey hair; who had so strong a will-power, too, and knitted such soft comforters "pour nos braves chers poilus." And suddenly she would say: "Madame n'est pas fatiguée?" And Madame would answer: "No. Speak English, Augustine—Polly will pick up your French! Come here!" And, reaching up a pale hand, she would set straight a stray fluff of the girl's dark-brown hair or improve the set of her fichu.

Those two got on extremely well, for though madame was—oh! but very particular, she was always "très gentille et toujours grande dame." And that love of form so deep in the French soul promoted the girl's admiration for one whom she could see would in no circumstances lose her dignity. Besides, Madame was full of dainty household devices, and could not bear waste; and these, though exacting, were qualities which appealed to Augustine. With her French passion for "the family" she used to wonder how in days like these Madame could endure to be far away from her son and daughter and the grandchildren, whose photographs hung on the walls; and the long letters her mistress was always writing in a beautiful, fine hand, beginning, "My darling Sybil," "My darling Reggie," and ending always "Your devoted mother," seemed to a warm and simple heart but meagre substitutes for flesh-and-blood realities. But as Madame would inform her—they were too busy doing things for the dear soldiers, and working for the war; they could not come to her—that would never do. And to go to them would give so much trouble, when the railways were so wanted for the troops; and she had their lovely letters, which she kept—as Augustine observed—every one in a lavender-scented sachet, and frequently took out to read. Another point of sympathy between those two was their passion for military music and seeing soldiers pass. Augustine's brother and father were at the front, and Madame's dead brother had been a soldier in the Crimean war—"long before you were born, Augustine, when the French and English fought the Russians; I was in France then, too, a little girl, and we lived at Nice; it was so lovely, you can't think—the flowers! And my poor brother was so cold in the siege of Sebastopol." Somehow, that time and that war were more real to her than this.

In December, when the hospitals were already full, her French friends first took her to the one which they attended. She went in, her face very calm, with that curious inward composure which never deserted it, carrying in front of her with both hands a black silk bag, wherein she had concealed an astonishing collection of treasures for the poor men! A bottle of acidulated drops, packets of cigarettes, two of her own mufflers, a pocket set of drafts, some English riddles translated by herself into French (very curious), some ancient copies of an illustrated paper, boxes of chocolate, a ball of string to make "cat's cradles" (such an amusing game), her own packs of Patience cards, some photograph frames, post-cards of Arles, and—most singular—a kettle-holder. At the head of each bed she would sit down and rummage in the bag, speaking in her slow but quite good French, to explain the use of the acidulated drops, or to give a lesson in cat's cradles. And the poilus would listen with their polite, ironic patience, and be left smiling, and curiously fascinated, as if they had been visited by a creature from another world. She would move on to other beds, quite unconscious of the effect she had produced on them and of their remarks: "Cette vieille dame, comme elle est bonne!" or "Espèce d'ange aux cheveux gris." "L'ange anglaise aux cheveux gris" became in fact her name within those walls. And the habit of filling that black silk bag and going there to distribute its contents soon grew to be with her a ruling passion which neither weather nor her own aches and pains, not inconsiderable, must interfere with. The things she brought became more marvellous every week. But, however much she carried coals to Newcastle, or tobacco pouches to those who did not smoke, or homoeopathic globules to such as crunched up the whole bottleful for the sake of the sugar, as soon as her back was turned, no one ever smiled now with anything but real pleasure at sight of her calm and truly sweet smile, and the scent of soap on her pale hands. "Cher fils, je croyais que ceci vous donnerait un peu de plaisir. Voyez-vous comme c'est commode, n'est ce pas?" Each newcomer to the wards was warned by his comrades that the English angel with the grey hair was to be taken without a smile, exactly as if she were his grandmother.

In the walk to the hospital Augustine would accompany her, carrying the bag and perhaps a large peasant's umbrella to cover them both, for the winter was hard and snowy, and carriages cost money, which must now be kept entirely for the almost daily replenishment of the bag and other calls of war. The girl, to her chagrin, was always left in a safe place, for it would never do to take her in and put fancies into her head, and perhaps excite the dear soldiers with a view of anything so taking. And when the visit was over they would set forth home, walking very slowly in the high, narrow streets, Augustine pouting a little and shooting swift glances at anything in uniform, and Madame making firm her lips against a fatigue which sometimes almost overcame her before she could get home and up the stairs. And the parrot would greet them indiscreetly with new phrases—"Keep smiling!" and "Kiss Augustine!" which he sometimes varied with "Kiss a poll, Poll!" or "Scratch Augustine!" to Madame's regret. Tea would revive her somewhat, and then she would knit, for as time went on and the war seemed to get farther and farther from that end which, in common with so many, she had expected before now, it seemed dreadful not to be always doing something to help the poor dear soldiers; and for dinner, to Augustine's horror, she now had nothing but a little soup, or an egg beaten up with milk and brandy. It saved such a lot of time and expense—she was sure people ate too much; and afterwards she would read the Daily Mail, often putting it down to sigh, and press her lips together, and think, "One must look on the bright side of things," and wonder a little where it was. And Augustine, finishing her work in the tiny kitchen, would sigh too, and think of red trousers and peaked caps, not yet out of date in that Southern region, and of her own heart saying "Kiss Augustine!" and she would peer out between the shutters at the stars sparkling over the Camargue, or look down where the ground fell away beyond an old, old wall, and nobody walked in the winter night, and muse on her nineteenth birthday coming, and sigh with the thought that she would be old before any one had loved her; and of how Madame was looking "très fatiguée."

Indeed, Madame was not merely looking "très fatiguée" in these days. The world's vitality and her own were at sad January ebb. But to think of oneself was quite impossible, of course; it would be all right presently, and one must not fuss, or mention in one's letters to the dear children that one felt at all poorly. As for a doctor—that would be sinful waste, and besides, what use were they except to tell you what you knew? So she was terribly vexed when Augustine found her in a faint one morning, and she found Augustine in tears, with her hair all over her face. She rated the girl soundly, but feebly, for making such a fuss over "a little thing like that," and with extremely trembling fingers pushed the brown hair back and told her to wash her face, while the parrot said reflectively: "Scratch a poll—Hullo!" The girl who had seen her own grandmother die not long before, and remembered how "fatiguée" she had been during her last days, was really frightened. Coming back after she had washed her face, she found her mistress writing on a number of little envelopes the same words: "En bonne Amitié." She looked up at the girl standing so ominously idle, and said:

"Take this hundred-franc note, Augustine, and go and get it changed into single francs—the ironmonger will do it if you say it's for me. I am going to take a rest. I sha'n't buy anything for the bag for a whole week. I shall just take francs instead."

"Oh, Madame! You must not go out: vous êtes trop fatiguée."

"Nonsense! How do you suppose our dear little Queen in England would get on with all she has to do, if she were to give in like that? We must none of us give up in these days. Help me to put on my things; I am going to church, and then I shall take a long rest before we go to the hospital."

"Oh, Madame! Must you go to church? It is not your kind of church. You do not pray there, do you?"

"Of course I pray there. I am very fond of the dear old church. God is in every church, Augustine; you ought to know that at your age."

"But Madame has her own religion?"

"Now, don't be silly. What does that matter? Help me into my cloth coat—not the fur—it's too heavy—and then go and get that money changed."

"But Madame should see a doctor. If Madame faints again I shall die with fright. Madame has no colour—but no colour at all; it must be that there is something wrong."

Madame rose, and taking the girl's ear between thumb and finger pinched it gently.

"You are a very silly girl. What would our poor soldiers do if all the nurses were like you?"

Reaching the church she sat down gladly, turning her face up towards her favourite picture, a Virgin standing with her Baby in her arms. It was only faintly coloured now; but there were those who said that an Arlésienne must have sat for it. Why it pleased her so she never quite knew, unless it were by its cool, unrestored devotion, by the faint smiling in the eyes. Religion with her was a strange yet very real thing. Conscious that she was not clever, she never even began to try and understand what she believed. Probably she believed nothing more than that if she tried to be good she would go to God—whatever and wherever God might be—some day when she was too tired to live any more; and rarely indeed did she forget to try to be good. As she sat there she thought, or perhaps prayed, whichever it should be called: "Let me forget that I have a body, and remember all the poor soldiers who have them."

It struck cold that morning in the church—the wind was bitter from the northeast; some poor women in black were kneeling, and four candles burned in the gloom of a side aisle—thin, steady little spires of gold. There was no sound at all. A smile came on her lips. She was forgetting that she had a body, and remembering all those young faces in the wards, the faces too of her own children far away, the faces of all she loved. They were real and she was not—she was nothing but the devotion she felt for them; yes, for all the poor souls on land and sea, fighting and working and dying. Her lips moved; she was saying below her breath, "I love them all"; then, feeling a shiver run down her spine, she compressed those lips and closed her eyes, letting her mind alone murmur her chosen prayer: "O God, who makes the birds sing and the stars shine, and gives us little children, strengthen my heart so that I may forget my own aches and wants and think of those of other people."

On reaching home again she took gelseminum, her favourite remedy against that shivering, which, however hard she tried to forget her own body, would keep coming; then, covering herself with her fur coat, she lay down, closing her eyes. She was seemingly asleep, so that Augustine, returning with the hundred single francs, placed them noiselessly beside the little pile of envelopes, and after looking at the white, motionless face of her mistress and shaking her own bonny head, withdrew. When she had gone, two tears came out of those closed eyes and clung on the pale cheeks below. The seeming sleeper was thinking of her children, away over there in England, her children and their children. Almost unbearably she was longing for a sight of them, not seen for so long now, recalling each face, each voice, each different way they had of saying, "Mother darling," or "Granny, look what I've got!" and thinking that if only the war would end how she would pack at once and go to them, that is, if they would not come to her for a nice long holiday in this beautiful place. She thought of spring, too, and how lovely it would be to see the trees come out again, and almond blossom against a blue sky. The war seemed so long, and winter too. But she must not complain; others had much greater sorrows than she—the poor widowed women kneeling in the church; the poor boys freezing in the trenches. God in his great mercy could not allow it to last much longer. It would not be like Him! Though she felt that it would be impossible to eat, she meant to force herself to make a good lunch so as to be able to go down as usual, and give her little presents. They would miss them so if she didn't. Her eyes, opening, rested almost gloatingly on the piles of francs and envelopes. And she began to think how she could reduce still further her personal expenditure. It was so dreadful to spend anything on oneself—an old woman like her. Doctor, indeed! If Augustine fussed any more she would send her away and do for herself! And the parrot, leaving his cage, which he could always do, perched just behind her and said: "Hullo! Kiss me, too!"

That afternoon in the wards every one noticed what a beautiful colour she had. "L'ange anglaise aux cheveux gris" had never been more popular. One poilu, holding up his envelope, remarked to his neighbour: "Elle verse des gouttes d'ciel, notr' 'tite gran'mè." To them, grateful even for those mysterious joys "cat's cradles," francs were the true drops from heaven.

She had not meant to give them all to-day, but it seemed dreadful, when she saw how pleased they were, to leave any out, and so the whole ninety-seven had their franc each. The three over would buy Augustine a little brooch to make up to the silly child for her fright in the morning. The buying of this brooch took a long time at the jeweller's in the rue des Romains, and she had only just fixed on an amethyst before feeling deadly ill with a dreadful pain through her lungs. She went out with her tiny package quickly, not wanting any fuss, and began to mount towards home. There were only three hundred yards to go, and with each step she said to herself: "Nonsense! What would the Queen think of you! Remember the poor soldiers with only one leg! You have got both your legs! And the poor men who walk from the battlefield with bullets through the lungs. What is your pain to theirs! Nonsense!" But the pain, like none she had ever felt—a pain which seemed to have sharp double edges like a knife— kept passing through and through her, till her legs had no strength at all, and seemed to move simply because her will said: "If you don't, I'll leave you behind. So there!" She felt as if perspiration were flowing down, yet her face was as dry as a dead leaf when she put up her hand to it. Her brain stammered; seemed to fly loose; came to sudden standstills. Her eyes searched painfully each grey-shuttered window for her own house, though she knew quite well that she had not reached it yet. From sheer pain she stood still, a wry little smile on her lips, thinking how poor Polly would say: "Keep smiling!" Then she moved on, holding out her hand, whether because she thought God would put his into it or only to pull on some imaginary rope to help her. So, foot by foot, she crept till she reached her door. A most peculiar floating sensation had come over her. The pain ceased, and as if she had passed through no doors, mounted no stairs—she was up in her room, lying on her sofa, with strange images about her, painfully conscious that she was not in proper control of her thoughts, and that Augustine must be thinking her ridiculous. Making a great effort, she said:

"I forbid you to send for a doctor, Augustine. I shall be all right in a day or two, if I eat plenty of francs. And you must put on this little brooch—I bought it for you from an angel in the street. Put my fur coat on Polly—he's shivering; dry your mouth, there's a good girl. Tell my son he mustn't think of leaving the poor War Office; I shall come and see him after the war. It will be over to-morrow, and then we will all go and have tea together in a wood. Granny will come to you, my darlings."

And when the terrified girl had rushed out she thought: "There, now she's gone to get God; and I mustn't disturb Him with all He has to see to. I shall get up and do for myself." When they came back with the doctor they found her half-dressed, trying to feed a perch in the empty cage with a spoon, and saying: "Kiss Granny, Polly. God is coming; kiss Granny!" while the parrot sat away over on the mantelpiece, with his head on one side, deeply interested.

When she had been properly undressed and made to lie down on the sofa, for she insisted so that she would not go to bed that they dared not oppose her, the doctor made his diagnosis. It was double pneumonia, of that sudden sort which declares for life or death in forty-eight hours. At her age a desperate case. Her children must be wired to at once. She had sunk back, seemingly unconscious; and Augustine, approaching the drawer where she knew the letters were kept, slipped out the lavender sachet and gave it to the doctor. When he had left the room to extract the addresses and send those telegrams, the girl sat down by the foot of the couch, leaning her elbows on her knees and her face on her hands, staring at that motionless form, while the tears streamed down her broad cheeks. For many minutes neither of them stirred, and the only sound was the restless stropping of the parrot's beak against a wire of his cage. Then her mistress's lips moved, and the girl bent forward. A whispering came forth, caught and suspended by breathless pausing:

"Mind, Augustine—no one is to tell my children—I can't have them disturbed—over a little thing—like this—and in my purse you'll find another—hundred-franc note. I shall want some more francs for the day after to-morrow. Be a good girl and don't fuss, and kiss poor Polly, and mind—I won't have a doctor—taking him away from his work. Give me my gelseminum and my prayer-book. And go to bed just as usual—we must all—keep smiling—like the dear soldiers—" The whispering ceased, then began again at once in rapid delirious incoherence. And the girl sat trembling, covering now her ears from those uncanny sounds, now her eyes from the flush and the twitching of that face, usually so pale and still. She could not follow—with her little English—the swerving, intricate flights of that old spirit mazed by fever—the memories released, the longings disclosed, the half-uttered prayers, the curious little half-conscious efforts to regain form and dignity. She could only pray to the Virgin. When relieved by the daughter of Madame's French friend, who spoke good English, she murmured desperately: "Oh! mademoiselle, madame est très fatiguée—la pauvre tête—faut-il enlever les cheveux? Elle fait ça toujours pour elle-même." For, to the girl, with her reverence for the fastidious dignity which never left her mistress, it seemed sacrilege to divest her of her crown of fine grey hair. Yet, when it was done and the old face crowned only by the thin white hair of nature, that dignity was still there surmounting the wandering talk and the moaning from her parched lips, which every now and then smiled and pouted in a kiss, as if remembering the maxims of the parrot. So the night passed, with all that could be done for her, whose most collected phrase, frequently uttered in the doctor's face, was: "Mind, Augustine, I won't have a doctor—I can manage for myself quite well." Once for a few minutes her spirit seemed to recover its coherence, and she was heard to whisper: "God has given me this so that I may know what the poor soldiers suffer. Oh! they've forgotten to cover Polly's cage." But high fever soon passes from the very old; and early morning brought a deathlike exhaustion, with utter silence, save for the licking of the flames at the olive-wood logs, and the sound as they slipped or settled down, calcined. The firelight crept fantastically about the walls covered with tapestry of French-grey silk, crept round the screen-head of the couch, and betrayed the ivory pallor of that mask-like face, which covered now such tenuous threads of life. Augustine, who had come on guard when the fever died away, sat in the armchair before those flames, trying hard to watch, but dropping off into the healthy sleep of youth. And out in the clear, hard shivering Southern cold, the old clocks chimed the hours into the winter dark, where, remote from man's restless spirit, the old town brooded above plain and river under the morning stars. And the girl dreamed—dreamed of a sweetheart under the acacias by her home, of his pinning their white flowers into her hair, till she woke with a little laugh. Light was already coming through the shutter chinks, the fire was but red embers and white ash. She gathered it stealthily together, put on fresh logs, and stole over to the couch. Oh! how white! how still! Was her mistress dead? The icy clutch of that thought jerked her hands up to her full breast, and a cry mounted in her throat. The eyes opened. The white lips parted, as if to smile; a voice whispered: "Now, don't be silly!" The girl's cry changed into a little sob, and bending down she put her lips to the ringed hand that lay outside the quilt. The hand moved faintly as if responding, the voice whispered: "The emerald ring is for you, Augustine. Is it morning? Uncover Polly's cage, and open his door."

Madame spoke no more that morning. A telegram had come. Her son and daughter would arrive next morning early. They waited for a moment of consciousness to tell her; but the day went by, and in spite of oxygen and brandy it did not come. She was sinking fast; her only movements were a tiny compression now and then of the lips, a half-opening of the eyes, and once a smile when the parrot spoke. The rally came at eight o'clock. Mademoiselle was sitting by the couch when the voice came fairly strong: "Give my love to my dear soldiers, and take them their francs out of my purse, please. Augustine, take care of Polly. I want to see if the emerald ring fits you. Take it off, please"; and, when it had been put on the little finger of the sobbing girl: "There, you see, it does. That's very nice. Your sweetheart will like that when you have one. What do you say, Mademoiselle? My son and daughter coming? All that way?" The lips smiled a moment, and then tears forced their way into her eyes. "My darlings! How good of them! Oh! what a cold journey they'll have! Get my room ready, Augustine, with a good fire! What are you crying for? Remember what Polly says: 'Keep smiling!' Think how bad it is for the poor soldiers if we women go crying! The Queen never cries, and she has ever so much to make her!"

No one could tell whether she knew that she was dying, except perhaps for those words, "Take care of Polly," and the gift of the ring.

She did not even seem anxious as to whether she would live to see her children. Her smile moved Mademoiselle to whisper to Augustine: "Elle a la sourire divine."

"Ah! mademoiselle, comme elle est brave, la pauvre dame! C'est qu'elle pense toujours aux autres." And the girl's tears dropped on the emerald ring.

Night fell—the long night; would she wake again? Both watched with her, ready at the faintest movement to administer oxygen and brandy. She was still breathing, but very faintly, when at six o'clock they heard the express come in, and presently the carriage stop before the house. Mademoiselle stole down to let them in.

Still in their travelling coats her son and daughter knelt down beside the couch, watching in the dim candle-light for a sign and cherishing her cold hands. Daylight came; they put the shutters back and blew out the candles. Augustine, huddled in the far corner, cried gently to herself. Mademoiselle had withdrawn. But the two still knelt, tears running down their cheeks. The face of their mother was so transparent, so exhausted; the least little twitching of just-opened lips showed that she breathed. A tiny sigh escaped; her eyelids fluttered. The son, leaning forward, said:

"Sweetheart, we're here."

The eyes opened then; something more than a simple human spirit seemed to look through—it gazed for a long, long minute; then the lips parted. They bent to catch the sound.

"My darlings—don't cry; smile!" And the eyes closed again. On her face a smile so touching that it rent the heart flickered and went out. Breath had ceased to pass the faded lips.

In the long silence the French girl's helpless sobbing rose; the parrot stirred uneasily in his still-covered cage. And the son and daughter knelt, pressing their faces hard against the couch.

CHAPTER II

DEFEAT

She had been standing there on the pavement a quarter of an hour or so after her shilling's worth of concert. Women of her profession are not supposed to have redeeming points, especially when—like

May Belinski, as she now preferred to dub herself—they are German; but this woman certainly had music in her soul. She often gave herself these "music baths" when the Promenade Concerts were on, and had just spent half her total wealth in listening to some Mozart and a Beethoven symphony.

She was feeling almost elated, full of divine sound, and of the wonderful summer moonlight which was filling the whole dark town. Women "of a certain type" have, at all events, emotions—and what a comfort that is, even to themselves! To stand just there had become rather a habit of hers. One could seem to be waiting for somebody coming out of the concert, not yet over—which, of course, was precisely what she was doing. One need not forever be stealthily glancing and perpetually moving on in that peculiar way, which, while it satisfied the police and Mrs. Grundy, must not quite deceive others as to her business in life. She had only "been at it" long enough to have acquired a nervous dread of almost everything—not long enough to have passed through that dread to callousness. Some women take so much longer than others. And even for a woman "of a certain type" her position was exceptionally nerve-racking in war-time, going as she did by a false name. Indeed, in all England there could hardly be a greater pariah than was this German woman of the night.

She idled outside a book-shop humming a little, pretending to read the titles of the books by moonlight, taking off and putting on one of her stained yellow gloves. Now and again she would move up as far as the posters outside the Hall, scrutinising them as if interested in the future, then stroll back again. In her worn and discreet dark dress, and her small hat, she had nothing about her to rouse suspicion, unless it were the trail of violet powder she left on the moonlight.

For the moonlight this evening was almost solid, seeming with its cool still vibration to replace the very air; in it the war-time precautions against light seemed fantastic, like shading candles in a room still full of daylight. What lights there were had the effect of strokes and stipples of dim colour laid by a painter's brush on a background of ghostly whitish blue. The dreamlike quality of the town was perhaps enhanced for her eyes by the veil she was wearing—in daytime no longer white. As the music died out of her, elation also ebbed. Somebody had passed her, speaking German, and she was overwhelmed by a rush of nostalgia. On this moonlight night by the banks of the Rhine—whence she came—the orchards would be heavy with apples; there would be murmurs, and sweet scents; the old castle would stand out clear, high over the woods and the chalky-white river. There would be singing far away, and the churning of a distant steamer's screw; and perhaps on the water a log raft still drifting down in the blue light. There would be German voices talking. And suddenly tears oozed up in her eyes, and crept down through the powder on her cheeks. She raised her veil and dabbed at her face with a little, not-too-clean handkerchief, screwed up in her yellow-gloved hand. But the more she dabbed, the more those treacherous tears ran. Then she became aware that a tall young man in khaki was also standing before the shop-window, not looking at the titles of the books, but eyeing her askance. His face was fresh and open, with a sort of kindly eagerness in his blue eyes. Mechanically she drooped her wet lashes, raised them obliquely, drooped them again, and uttered a little sob....

This young man, Captain in a certain regiment, and discharged from hospital at six o'clock that evening, had entered Queen's Hall at half-past seven. Still rather brittle and sore from his wound, he had treated himself to a seat in the Grand Circle, and there had sat, very still and dreamy, the whole concert through. It had been like eating after a long fast—something of the sensation Polar explorers must experience when they return to their first full meal. For he was of the New Army, and before the war had actually believed in music, art, and all that sort of thing. With a month's leave before him, he could afford to feel that life was extraordinarily joyful, his own experiences particularly wonderful; and, coming out into the moonlight, he had taken what can only be described as a great gulp of it, for he was a young man with a sense of beauty. When one has been long in the trenches, lain out wounded in a shell-hole twenty-four hours, and spent three months in hospital, beauty has such an edge of novelty, such a sharp sweetness, that it almost gives pain. And London at night is very beautiful. He strolled slowly towards the Circus, still drawing the moonlight deep into his lungs, his cap tilted up a little on his forehead in that moment of unmilitary abandonment; and whether he stopped before the book-shop window because the girl's figure was in some sort a part of beauty, or because he saw that she was crying, he could not have made clear to any one.

Then something—perhaps the scent of powder, perhaps the yellow glove, or the oblique flutter of the eyelids—told him that he was making what he would have called "a blooming error," unless he wished for company, which had not been in his thoughts. But her sob affected him, and he said:

"What's the matter?"

Again her eyelids fluttered sideways, and she stammered:

"Not'ing. The beautiful evening—that's why!"

That a woman of what he now clearly saw to be "a certain type" should perceive what he himself had just been perceiving, struck him forcibly, and he said:

"Cheer up."

She looked up again swiftly: "Cheer up! You are not lonelee like me."

For one of that sort, she looked somehow honest; her tear-streaked face was rather pretty, and he murmured:

"Well, let's walk a bit, and talk it over."

They turned the corner, and walked east, along streets empty, and beautiful, with their dulled orange-glowing lamps, and here and there the glint of some blue or violet light. He found it queer and rather exciting—for an adventure of just this kind he had never had. And he said doubtfully:

"How did you get into this? Isn't it an awfully hopeless sort of life?"

"Ye-es, it ees—" her voice had a queer soft emphasis. "You are limping—haf you been wounded?"

"Just out of hospital to-day."

"The horrible war—all the misery is because of the war. When will it end?"

He looked at her attentively, and said:

"I say—what nationality are you?"

"Rooshian."

"Really! I never met a Russian girl."

He was conscious that she looked at him, then very quickly down. And he said suddenly:

"Is it as bad as they make out?"

She slipped her yellow-gloved hand through his arm.

"Not when I haf any one as nice as you; I never haf yet, though"; she smiled—and her smile was like her speech, slow, confiding—"you stopped because I was sad, others stop because I am gay. I am not fond of men at all. When you know, you are not fond of them."

"Well! You hardly know them at their best, do you? You should see them at the front. By George! they're simply splendid—officers and men, every blessed soul. There's never been anything like it—just one long bit of jolly fine self-sacrifice; it's perfectly amazing."

Turning her blue-grey eyes on him, she answered:

"I expect you are not the last at that. You see in them what you haf in yourself, I think."

"Oh! not a bit—you're quite out. I assure you when we made the attack where I got wounded, there wasn't a single man in my regiment who wasn't an absolute hero. The way they went in—never thinking of themselves—it was simply superb!"

Her teeth came down on her lower lip, and she answered in a queer voice: "It is the same too perhaps with—the enemy."

"Oh yes, I know that."

"Ah! You are not a mean man. How I hate mean men!"

"Oh! they're not mean really—they simply don't understand."

"Oh! you are a baby—a good baby, aren't you?"

He did not quite like being called a baby, and frowned; but was at once touched by the disconcertion in her powdered face. How quickly she was scared!

She said clingingly:

"But I li-ike you for it. It is so good to find a ni-ice man."

This was worse, and he said abruptly:

"About being lonely? Haven't you any Russian friends?"

"Rooshian! No!" Then quickly added: "The town is so beeg! Haf you been in the concert?"

"Yes."

"I, too—I love music."

"I suppose all Russians do."

She looked up at his face again, and seemed to struggle to keep silent; then she said quietly:

"I go there always when I haf the money."

"What! Are you so on the rocks?"

"Well, I haf just one shilling now." And she laughed.

The sound of that little laugh upset him—she had a way of making him feel sorry for her every time she spoke.

They had come by now to a narrow square, east of Gower Street.

"This is where I lif," she said. "Come in!"

He had one long moment of violent hesitation, then yielded to the soft tugging of her hand, and followed. The passage-hall was dimly lighted, and they went upstairs into a front room, where the curtains were drawn, and the gas turned very low. Opposite the window were other curtains dividing off the rest of the apartment. As soon as the door was shut she put up her face and kissed him—evidently formula. What a room! Its green and beetroot colouring and the prevalence of cheap plush disagreeably affected him. Everything in it had that callous look of rooms which seem to be saying to their occupants: "You're here to-day and you'll be gone to-morrow." Everything except one little plant, in a common pot, of maidenhair fern, fresh and green, looking as if it had been watered within the hour; in this room it had just the same unexpected touchingness that peeped out of the girl's matter-of-fact cynicism.

Taking off her hat, she went towards the gas, but he said quickly:

"No, don't turn it up; let's have the window open, and the moonlight in." He had a sudden dread of seeing anything plainly—it was stuffy, too, and pulling the curtains apart, he threw up the window. The girl had come obediently from the hearth, and sat down opposite him, leaning her arm on the window-sill and her chin on her hand. The moonlight caught her cheek where she had just renewed the powder, caught her fair crinkly hair; it caught the plush of the furniture, and his own khaki, giving them all a touch of unreality.

"What's your name?" he said.

"May. Well, I call myself that. It's no good askin' yours."

"You're a distrustful little party, aren't you?"

"I haf reason to be, don't you think?"

"Yes, I suppose you're bound to think us all brutes?"

"Well, I haf a lot of reasons to be afraid all my time. I am dreadfully nervous now; I am not trusting anybody. I suppose you haf been killing lots of Germans?"

He laughed.

"We never know, unless it happens to be hand to hand; I haven't come in for that yet."

"But you would be very glad if you had killed some?"

"Glad? I don't think so. We're all in the same boat, so far as that's concerned. We're not glad to kill each other. We do our job—that's all."

"Oh! it is frightful. I expect I haf my broders killed."

"Don't you get any news ever?"

"News! No indeed, no news of anybody in my country. I might not haf a country; all that I ever knew is gone—fader, moder, sisters, broders, all—never any more I shall see them, I suppose, now. The war it breaks and breaks, it breaks hearts." Her little teeth fastened again on her lower lip in that sort of pretty snarl. "Do you know what I was thinkin' when you came up? I was thinkin' of my native town, and the river there in the moonlight. If I could see it again, I would be glad. Were you ever homeseeck?"

"Yes, I have been—in the trenches; but one's ashamed, with all the others."

"Ah! ye-es!" It came from her with a hiss. "Ye-es! You are all comrades there. What is it like for me here, do you think, where everybody hates and despises me, and would catch me, and put me in prison, perhaps?"

He could see her breast heaving with a quick breathing painful to listen to. He leaned forward, patting her knee, and murmuring: "Sorry—sorry."

She said in a smothered voice:

"You are the first who has been kind to me for so long! I will tell you the truth—I am not Rooshian at all—I am German."

Hearing that half-choked confession, his thought was: "Does she really think we fight against women?" And he said:

"My dear girl, who cares?"

Her eyes seemed to search right into him. She said slowly:

"Another man said that to me. But he was thinkin' of other things. You are a veree ni-ice boy. I am so glad I met you. You see the good in people, don't you? That is the first thing in the world—because there is really not much good in people, you know."

He said, smiling:

"You're a dreadful little cynic!" Then thought: "Of course she is—poor thing!"

"Cyneec? How long do you think I would live if I was not a cyneec? I should drown myself to-morrow. Perhaps there are good people, but, you see, I don't know them."

"I know lots."

She leaned forward eagerly.

"Well now—see, ni-ice boy—you haf never been in a hole, haf you?"

"I suppose not a real hole."

"No, I should think not, with your face. Well, suppose I am still a good girl, as I was once, you know, and you took me to some of your good people, and said: 'Here is a little German girl that has no work, and no money, and no friends.' Your good people they will say: 'Oh! how sad! A German girl!' and they will go and wash their hands."

Silence fell on him. He saw his mother, his sisters, others—good people, he would swear! And yet—! He heard their voices, frank and clear; and they seemed to be talking of the Germans. If only she were not German!

"You see!" he heard her say, and could only mutter:

"I'm sure there are people."

"No. They would not take a German, even if she was good. Besides, I don't want to be good any more—I am not a humbug—I have learned to be bad. Aren't you going to kees me, ni-ice boy?"

She put her face close to his. Her eyes troubled him, but he drew back. He thought she would be offended or persistent, but she was neither; just looked at him fixedly with a curious inquiring stare; and he leaned against the window, deeply disturbed. It was as if all clear and simple enthusiasm had been suddenly knocked endways; as if a certain splendour of life that he had felt and seen of late had been dipped in cloud. Out there at the front, over here in hospital, life had been seeming so—as it were—heroic; and yet it held such mean and murky depths as well! The voices of his men, whom he had come to love like brothers, crude burring voices, cheery in trouble, making nothing of it; the voices of doctors and nurses, patient, quiet, reassuring voices; even his own voice, infected by it all, kept sounding in his ears. All wonderful somehow, and simple; and nothing mean about it anywhere! And now so suddenly to have lighted upon this, and all that was behind it—this scared girl, this base, dark, thoughtless use of her! And the thought came to him: "I suppose my fellows wouldn't think twice about taking her on! Why! I'm not even certain of myself, if she insists!" And he turned his face, and stared out at the moonlight. He heard her voice:

"Eesn't it light? No air raid to-night. When the Zepps burned—what a horrible death! And all the people cheered—it is natural. Do you hate us veree much?"

He turned round and said sharply:

"Hate? I don't know."

"I don't hate even the English—I despise them. I despise my people too—perhaps more, because they began this war. Oh, yes! I know that. I despise all the peoples. Why haf they made the world so miserable—why haf they killed all our lives—hundreds and thousands and millions of lives—all for not'ing? They haf made a bad world—everybody hating, and looking for the worst everywhere. They haf made me bad, I know. I believe no more in anything. What is there to believe in? Is there a God? No! Once I was teaching little English children their prayers—isn't that funnee? I was reading to them about Christ and love. I believed all those things. Now I believe not'ing at all—no one who is not a fool or a liar can believe. I would like to work in a hospital; I would like to go and help poor boys like you. Because I am a German they would throw me out a hundred times, even if I was good. It is the same in Germany and France and Russia, everywhere. But do you think I will believe in love and Christ and a God and all that?—not I! I think we are animals—that's all! Oh! yes—you fancy it is because my life has spoiled me. It is not that at all—that's not the worst thing in life. Those men are not ni-ice, like you, but it's their nature, and," she laughed, "they help me to live, which is something for me anyway. No, it is the men who think themselves great and good, and make the war with their talk and their hate, killing us all—killing all the boys like you, and keeping poor people in prison, and telling us to go on hating; and all those dreadful cold-blooded creatures who write in the papers—the same in my country, just the same; it is because of all them that I think we are only animals."

He got up, acutely miserable. He could see her following him with her eyes, and knew she was afraid she had driven him away. She said coaxingly: "Don't mind me talking, ni-ice boy. I don't know any one to talk to. If you don't like it, I can be quiet as a mouse."

He muttered:

"Oh! go on, talk away. I'm not obliged to believe you, and I don't."

She was on her feet now, leaning against the wall; her dark dress and white face just touched by the slanting moonlight; and her voice came again, slow and soft and bitter:

"Well, look here, ni-ice boy, what sort of a world is it, where millions are being tortured—horribly tortured, for no fault of theirs, at all? A beautiful world, isn't it! 'Umbug! Silly rot, as you boys call it. You say it is all 'Comrade'! and braveness out there at the front, and people don't think of themselves. Well, I don't think of myself veree much. What does it matter—I am lost now, anyway; but I think of my people at home, how they suffer and grieve. I think of all the poor people there and here who lose those they love, and all the poor prisoners. Am I not to think of them? And if I do, how am I to believe it a beautiful world, ni-ice boy?"

He stood very still, biting his lips.

"Look here! We haf one life each, and soon it is over. Well, I think that is lucky."

He said resentfully:

"No! there's more than that."

"Ah!" she went on softly; "you think the war is fought for the future; you are giving your lives for a better world, aren't you?"

"We must fight till we win," he said between his teeth.

"Till you win. My people think that, too. All the peoples think that if they win the world will be better. But it will not, you know, it will be much worse, anyway."

He turned away from her and caught up his cap; but her voice followed him.

"I don't care which win, I despise them all—animals—animals—animals! Ah! Don't go, ni-ice boy—I will be quiet now."

He took some notes from his tunic pocket, put them on the table, and went up to her.

"Good-night."

She said plaintively:

"Are you really going? Don't you like me, enough?"

"Yes, I like you."

"It is because I am German, then?"

"No."

"Then why won't you stay?"

He wanted to answer: "Because you upset me so"; but he just shrugged his shoulders.

"Won't you kees me once?"

He bent, and put his lips to her forehead; but as he took them away she threw her head back, pressed her mouth to his, and clung to him.

He sat down suddenly and said:

"Don't! I don't want to feel a brute."

She laughed. "You are a funny boy, but you are veree good. Talk to me a little, then. No one talks to me. I would much rather talk, anyway. Tell me, haf you seen many German prisoners?"

He sighed—from relief, or was it from regret?

"A good many."

"Any from the Rhine?"

"Yes, I think so."

"Were they very sad?"

"Some were—some were quite glad to be taken."

"Did you ever see the Rhine? Isn't it beauiful? It will be wonderful to-night. The moonlight will be the same here as there; in Rooshia too, and France, everywhere; and the trees will look the same as here, and people will meet under them and make love just as here. Oh! isn't it stupid, the war?—as if it was not good to be alive."

He wanted to say: "You can't tell how good it is to be alive, till you're facing death, because you don't live till then. And when a whole lot of you feel like that—and are ready to give their lives for each other, it's worth all the rest of life put together." But he couldn't get it out to this girl who believed in nothing.

"How were you wounded, ni-ice boy?"

"Attacking across open ground—four machine-gun bullets got me at one go off."

"Weren't you veree frightened when they ordered you to attack?" No, he had not been frightened just then! And he shook his head and laughed.

"It was great. We did laugh that morning. They got me much too soon, though—a swindle!"

She stared at him.

"You laughed?"

"Yes, and what do you think was the first thing I was conscious of next morning—my old Colonel bending over me and giving me a squeeze of lemon. If you knew my Colonel you'd still believe in things. There is something, you know, behind all this evil. After all, you can only die once, and if it's for your country all the better."

Her face, with intent eyes just touched with bistre, had in the moonlight a most strange, otherworld look. Her lips moved:

"No, I believe in nothing. My heart is dead."

"You think so, but it isn't, you know, or you wouldn't have been crying, when I met you."

"If it were not dead, do you think I could live my life—walking the streets every night, pretending to like strange men—never hearing a kind word—never talking, for fear I will be known for a German. Soon I shall take to drinking, then I shall be 'Kaput' very quick. You see, I am practical, I see things clear. To-night I am a little emotional; the moon is funny, you know. But I live for myself only, now. I don't care for anything or anybody."

"All the same, just now you were pitying your people, and prisoners, and that."

"Yes, because they suffer. Those who suffer are like me—I pity myself, that's all; I am different from your Englishwomen. I see what I am doing; I do not let my mind become a turnip just because I am no longer moral."

"Nor your heart either."

"Ni-ice boy, you are veree obstinate. But all that about love is 'umbug. We love ourselves, nothing more."

Again, at that intense soft bitterness in her voice, he felt stifled, and got up, leaning in the window. The air out there was free from the smell of dust and stale perfume. He felt her fingers slip between his own, and stay unmoving. Since she was so hard, and cynical, why should he pity her? Yet he did. The touch of that hand within his own roused his protective instinct. She had poured out her heart to him—a perfect stranger! He pressed it a little, and felt her fingers crisp in answer. Poor girl! This was perhaps a friendlier moment than she had known for years! And after all, fellow-feeling was bigger than principalities and powers! Fellow-feeling was all-pervading as this moonlight, which she had said would be the same in Germany—as this white ghostly glamour that wrapped the trees, making the orange lamps so quaint and decoratively useless out in the narrow square, where emptiness and silence reigned. He looked around into her face—in spite of bistre and powder, and the faint rouging on her lips, it had a queer, unholy, touching beauty. And he had suddenly the strangest feeling, as if they stood there—the two of them—proving that kindness and human fellowship were stronger than lust, stronger than hate; proving it against meanness and brutality, and the sudden shouting of newspaper boys in some neighbouring street. Their cries, passionately vehement, clashed into each other, and obscured the words—what was it they were calling? His head went up to listen; he felt her hand rigid within his arm—she too was listening. The cries came nearer, hoarser, more shrill and clamorous; the empty moonlight seemed of a sudden crowded with footsteps, voices, and a fierce distant cheering. "Great victory—great victory! Official! British! Defeat of the 'Uns! Many thousand prisoners!" So it sped by, intoxicating, filling him with a fearful joy; and leaning far out, he waved his cap and cheered like a madman; and the whole night seemed to him to flutter and vibrate, and answer. Then he turned to rush down into the street, struck against something soft, and recoiled. The girl! She stood with hands clenched, her face convulsed, panting, and even in the madness of his joy he felt for her. To hear this— in the midst of enemies! All confused with the desire to do something, he stooped to take her hand; and the dusty reek of the table-cloth clung to his nostrils. She snatched away her fingers, swept up the notes he had put down, and held them out to him.

"Take them—I will not haf your English money—take them." And suddenly she tore them across twice, three times, let the bits flutter to the floor, and turned her back to him. He stood looking at her leaning against the plush-covered table which smelled of dust; her head down, a dark figure in a dark room with the moonlight sharpening her outline—hardly a moment he stayed, then made for the door....

When he was gone she still stood there, her chin on her breast—she who cared for nothing, believed in nothing—with the sound in her ears of cheering, of hurrying feet, and voices; stood, in the centre of a pattern made by fragments of the torn-up notes, staring out into the moonlight, seeing, not this hated room and the hated square outside, but a German orchard, and herself, a little girl, plucking apples, a big dog beside her; a hundred other pictures, too, such as the drowning see. Her heart swelled; she sank down on the floor, laid her forehead on the dusty carpet, and pressed her body to it.

She who did not care—who despised all peoples, even her own—began, mechanically, to sweep together the scattered fragments of the notes, assembling them with the dust into a little pile, as of fallen leaves, and dabbling in it with her fingers, while the tears ran down her cheeks. For her country she had torn them, her country in defeat! She, who had just one shilling in this great town of enemies, who wrung her stealthy living out of the embraces of her foes! And suddenly in the moonlight she sat up and began to sing with all her might—"Die Wacht am Rhein."

CHAPTER III

FLOTSAM AND JETSAM

A REMINISCENCE

The tides of the war were washing up millions of wrecked lives on all the shores; what mattered the flotsam of a conscripted deep-sea Breton fisherman, slowly pining away for lack of all he was accustomed to; or the jetsam of a tall glass-blower from the 'invaded countries,' drifted into the hospital—no one quite knew why—prisoner for twenty months with the Boches, released at last because of his half-paralysed tongue—What mattered they? What mattered anything, or any one, in days like those?

Corporal Mignan, wrinkling a thin, parchmenty face, full of suffering and kindly cynicism, used to call them 'mes deux phénomènes.' Riddled to the soul by gastritis, he must have found them trying roommates, with the tricks and manners of sick and naughty children towards a long-suffering nurse. To understand all is to forgive all, they say; but, though he had suffered enough to understand much, Mignan was tempted at times to deliver judgment—for example, when Roche, the Breton fisherman, rose from his bed more than ten times in the night, and wandered out into the little courtyard of the hospital, to look at the stars, because he could not keep still within four walls—so unreasonable of the 'type.' Or when Gray, the tall glass-blower—his grandfather had been English—refused with all the tenacity of a British workman to wear an undervest, with the thermometer below zero, Centigrade.

They inhabited the same room, Flotsam and Jetsam, but never spoke to one another. And yet in all that hospital of French soldiers they were the only two who, in a manner of speaking, had come from England. Fourteen hundred years have passed since the Briton ancestors of Roche crossed in their shallow boats. Yet he was as hopelessly un-French as a Welshman of the hills is to this day un-English. His dark face, shy as a wild animal's, his peat-brown eyes, and the rare, strangely-sweet smile which once in a way strayed up into them; his creased brown hands always trying to tie an imaginary cord; the tobacco pouched in his brown cheek; his improperly-buttoned blue trousers; his silence eternal as the stars themselves; his habit of climbing trees—all marked him out as no true Frenchman. Indeed, that habit of climbing trees caused every soul who saw him to wonder if he ought to be at large: monkeys alone pursue this pastime. And yet,—surely one might understand that trees were for Roche the masts of his far-off fishing barque, each hand-grip on the branch of plane or pine-tree solace to his overmastering hunger for the sea. Up there he would cling, or stand with hands in pockets, and look out, far over the valley and the yellowish-grey-pink of the pan-tiled town-roofs, a mile away, far into the mountains where snow melted not, far over this foreign land of 'midi trois quarts,' to an imagined Breton coast and the seas that roll from there to Cape Breton where the cod are. Since he never spoke unless spoken to—no, not once—it was impossible for his landsmen comrades to realise why he got up those trees, and they would summon each other to observe this 'phénomène,' this human ourang-outang, who had not their habit of keeping firm earth beneath their feet. They understood his other eccentricities better. For instance, he could not stay still even at his meals, but must get up and slip out, because he chewed tobacco, and, since the hospital regulations forbade his spitting on the floor, he must naturally go and spit outside. For 'ces types-la' to chew and drink was—life! To the presence of tobacco in the cheek and the absence of drink from the stomach they attributed all his un-French ways, save just that one mysterious one of climbing trees.

And Gray—though only one-fourth English—how utterly British was that 'arrogant civilian,' as the 'poilus' called him. Even his clothes, somehow, were British—no one knew who had given them to him; his short grey workman's jacket, brown dingy trousers, muffler and checked cap; his long, idle walk, his absolute sans-gêne, regardless of any one but himself; his tall, loose figure, with a sort of grace lurking somewhere in its slow, wandering movements, and long, thin fingers. That wambling, independent form might surely be seen any day outside a thousand British public-houses, in time of peace. His face, with its dust-coloured hair, projecting ears, grey eyes with something of the child in them, and something of the mule, and something of a soul trying to wander out of the forest of misfortune; his little, tip-tilted nose that never grew on pure-blooded Frenchman; under a scant moustache his thick lips, disfigured by infirmity of speech, whence passed so continually a dribble of saliva—sick British workman was stamped on him. Yet he was passionately fond of washing himself; his teeth, his head, his clothes. Into the frigid winter he would go, and stand at the 'Source' half an hour at a time, washing and washing. It was a cause of constant irritation to Mignan that his 'phénomène' would never come to time, on account of this disastrous habit; the hospital corridors resounded almost daily with the importuning of those shapeless lips for something clean—a shirt, a pair of drawers, a bath, a handkerchief. He had a fixity of purpose; not too much purpose, but so fixed.—Yes, he was English!

For 'les deux phénomènes' the soldiers, the servants, and the 'Powers' of the hospital—all were sorry; yet they could not understand to the point of quite forgiving their vagaries. The twain were outcast, wandering each in a dumb world of his own, each in the endless circle of one or two hopeless notions. It was irony—or the French system—which had ordered the Breton Roche to get well in a place whence he could see nothing flatter than a mountain, smell no sea, eat no fish. And God knows what had sent Gray there. His story was too vaguely understood, for his stumbling speech simply could not make it plain. 'Les Boches—ils vont en payer cher—les Boches,' muttered fifty times a day, was the burden of his song. Those Boches had come into his village early in the war, torn him from his wife and his 'petite fille.' Since then he had 'had fear,' been hungry, been cold, eaten grass; eyeing some fat little dog, he would leer and mutter: 'J'ai mangé cela, c'est bon!' and with fierce triumph add: 'Ils ont faim, les Boches!' The 'arrogant civilian' had never done his military service, for his infirmity, it seemed, had begun before the war.

Dumb, each in his own way, and differing in every mortal thing except the reality of their misfortunes, never were two beings more lonely. Their quasi-nurse, Corporal Mignan, was no doubt right in his estimate of their characters. For him, so patient in the wintry days, with his 'deux phénomènes,' they were divested of all that halo which misfortune sets round the heads of the afflicted. He had too much to do with them, and saw them as they would have been if undogged by Fate. Of Roche he would say: 'Il n'est pas mon rêve. Je n'aime pas ces types taciturnes; quand même, il n'est pas mauvais. Il est marin—les marins—!' and he would shrug his shoulders, as who should say: 'Those poor devils—what can you expect?' 'Mais ce Gray'—it was one bitter day when Gray had refused absolutely to wear his great-coat during a motor drive—'c'est un mauvais type! Il est malin—il sait très bien ce qu'il veut. C'est un egoiste!' An egoist! Poor Gray! No doubt he was, instinctively conscious that if he did not make the most of what little personality was left within his wandering form, it would slip and he would be no more. Even a winter fly is mysteriously anxious not to become dead. That he was 'malin'—cunning—became the accepted view about Gray; not so 'malin' that he could 'cut three paws off a duck,' as the old grey Territorial, Grandpère Poirot, would put it, but 'malin' enough to know very well what he wanted, and how, by sticking to his demand, to get it. Mignan, typically French, did not allow enough for the essential Englishman in Gray. Besides, one must be malin if one has only the power to say about one-tenth of what one wants, and then not be understood once in twenty times. Gray did not like his great-coat—a fine old French-blue military thing with brass buttons—the arrogant civilian would have none of it! It was easier to shift the Boches on the Western front than to shift an idea, once in his head. In the poor soil of his soul the following plants of thought alone now flourished: Hatred of the Boches; love of English tobacco—'Il est bon—il est bon!' he would say, tapping his Virginian cigarette; the wish to see again his 'petite fille'; to wash himself; to drink a 'café natur' and bottled beer every day after the midday meal, and to go to Lyons to see his uncle and work for his living. And who shall say that any of these fixed ideas were evil in him?

But back to Flotsam, whose fixed idea was Brittany! Nostalgia is a long word, and a malady from which the English do not suffer, for they carry their country on their backs, walk the wide world in a cloud of their own atmosphere, making that world England. The French have eyes to see, and, when not surrounded by houses that have flatness, shutters, and subtle colouring—yellowish, French-grey, French-green—by café's, by plane-trees, by Frenchwomen, by scents of wood-smoke and coffee roasted in the streets; by the wines, and infusions of the herbs of France; by the churches of France and the beautiful silly chiming of their bells—when not surrounded by all these, they know it, feel it, suffer. But even they do not suffer so dumbly and instinctively, so like a wild animal caged, as that Breton fisherman, caged up in a world of hill and valley—not the world as he had known it. They called his case 'shell-shock'—for the French system would not send a man to convalescence for anything so essentially civilian as home-sickness, even when it had taken a claustrophobic turn. A system recognises only causes which you can see; holes in the head, hamstrung legs, frostbitten feet, with other of the legitimate consequences of war. But it was not shell-shock. Roche was really possessed by the feeling that he would never get out, never get home, smell fish and the sea, watch the bottle-green breakers roll in on his native shore, the sun gleaming through wave-crests lifted and flying back in spray, never know the accustomed heave and roll under his feet, or carouse in a seaport cabaret, or see his old mother—la veuve Roche. And, after all, there was a certain foundation for his fear. It was not as if this war could be expected to stop some day. There they were, in the trenches, they and the enemy set over against each other, 'like china dogs,' in the words of Grandpère Poirot; and there they would be, so far as Roche's ungeared nerves could grasp, for ever. And, while like china dogs they sat, he knew that he would not be released, not allowed to go back to the sea and the smells and the sounds thereof; for he had still all his limbs, and no bullet-hole to show under his thick dark hair. No wonder he got up the trees and looked out for sight of the waves, and fluttered the weak nerves of the hospital 'Powers,' till they saw themselves burying him with a broken spine, at the expense of the subscribers. Nothing to be done for the poor fellow, except to take him motor-drives, and to insist that he stayed in the dining-room long enough to eat some food.

Then, one bright day, a 'Power,' watching his hands, conceived the idea of giving him two balls of string, one blue, the other buff, and all that afternoon he stayed up a single tree, and came down with one of his rare sweet smiles and a little net, half blue, half buff, with a handle covered with a twist of Turkey-red twill—such a thing as one scoops up shrimps with. He was paid for it, and his eyes sparkled. You see, he had no money—the 'poilu' seldom has; and money meant drink, and tobacco in his cheek. They gave him more string, and for the next few days it rained little nets, beautifully if simply made. They thought that his salvation was in sight. It takes an eye to tell salvation from damnation, sometimes.... In any case, he no longer roamed from tree to tree, but sat across a single branch, netting. The 'Powers' began to speak of him as 'rather a dear,' for it is characteristic of human nature to take interest only in that which by some sign of progress makes you feel that you are doing good.

Next Sunday a distinguished doctor came, and, when he had been fed, some one conceived the notion of interesting him, too, in Flotsam. A learned, kindly, influential man—well-fed—something might come of it, even that 'réforme,' that sending home, which all agreed was what poor Roche needed, to restore his brain. He was brought in, therefore, amongst the chattering party, and stood, dark, shy, his head down, like the man in Millet's 'Angelus,' his hands folded on his cap, in front of his unspeakably buttoned blue baggy trousers, as though in attitude of prayer to the doctor, who, uniformed and grey-bearded, like an old somnolent goat, beamed on him through spectacles with a sort of shrewd benevolence. The catechism began. So he had something to ask, had he? A swift, shy lift of the eyes: 'Yes.' 'What then?' 'To go home.' 'To go home? What for? To get married?' A swift, shy smile. 'Fair or dark?' No answer, only a shift of hands on his cap. 'What! Was there no one—no ladies at home?' 'Ce n'est pas ça qui manque!' At the laughter greeting that dim flicker of wit the uplifted face was cast down again. That lonely, lost figure must suddenly have struck the doctor, for his catechism became a long, embarrassed scrutiny; and with an: 'Eh bien! mon vieux, nous verrons!' ended. Nothing came of it, of course. 'Cas de réforme?' Oh, certainly, if it had depended on the learned, kindly doctor. But the system—and all its doors to be unlocked! Why, by the time the last door was prepared to open, the first would be closed again! So the 'Powers' gave Roche more string—so good, you know, to see him interested in something!... It does take an eye to tell salvation from damnation! For he began to go down now of an afternoon into the little old town—not smelless, but most quaint—all yellowish-grey, with rosy-tiled roofs. Once it had been Roman, once a walled city of the Middle Ages; never would it be modern. The dogs ran muzzled; from a first-floor a goat, munching green fodder, hung his devilish black beard above your head; and through the main street the peasant farmers, above military age, looking old as sun-dried roots, in their dark pélerines, drove their wives and produce in little slow carts. Parched oleanders in pots one would pass, and old balconies with wilting flowers hanging down over the stone, and perhaps an umbrella with a little silver handle, set out to dry. Roche would go in by the back way, where the old town gossips sat on a bench in the winter sunshine, facing the lonely cross shining gold on the high hill-top opposite, placed there in days when there was some meaning in such things; past the little 'Place' with the old fountain and the brown plane-trees in front of the Mairie; past the church, so ancient that it had fortunately been forgotten, and remained unfinished and beautiful. Did Roche, Breton that he was—half the love-ladies in Paris, they say—falsely, no doubt—are Bretonnes—ever enter the church in passing? Some rascal had tried to burn down its beautiful old door from the inside, and the flames had left on all that high western wall smears like the fingermarks of hell, or the background of a Velasquez Crucifixion. Did he ever enter and stand, knotting his knot which never got knotted, in the dark loveliness of that grave building, where in the deep silence a dusty-gold little angel blows on his horn from the top of the canopied pulpit, and a dim carved Christ of touching beauty looks down on His fellow-men from above some dry chrysanthemums; and a tall candle burned quiet and lonely here and there, and the flags of France hung above the altar, that men might know how God— though resting—was with them and their country? Perhaps! But, more likely, he passed it, with its great bell riding high and open among scrolls of ironwork, and—Breton that he was—entered the nearest cabaret, kept by the woman who would tell you that her soldier husband had passed 'within two fingers' of death. One cannot spend one's earnings in a church, nor appease there the inextinguishable longings of a sailor.

And lo!—on Christmas day Roche came back so drunk that his nurse Mignan took him to his bedroom and turned the key of the door on him. But you must not do this to a Breton fisherman full of drink and claustrophobia. It was one of those errors even Frenchmen may make, to the after sorrow of their victims. One of the female 'Powers,' standing outside, heard a roar, the crash of a foot against the panel of a door, and saw Roche, 'like a great cat' come slithering through the hole. He flung his arm out, brushed the 'Power' back against the wall, cried out fiercely: 'La boîte—je ne veux pas la boîte!' and rushed for the stairs. Here were other female 'Powers'; he dashed them aside and passed down. But in the bureau at the foot was a young Corporal of the 'Legion Etrangère'—a Spaniard who had volunteered for France—great France; he ran out, took Roche gently by the arm, and offered to drink with him. And so they sat, those two, in the little bureau, drinking black coffee, while the young Corporal talked like an angel and Roche like a wild man—about his mother, about his dead brother who had been sitting on his bed, as he said, about 'la boîte,' and the turning of that key. And slowly he became himself—or so they thought—and all went in to supper. Ten minutes later one of the 'Powers,' looking for the twentieth time to make sure he was eating, saw an empty place: he had slipped out like a shadow and was gone again. A big cavalryman and the Corporal retrieved him that night from a café near the station; they had to use force at times to bring him in. Two days later he was transferred to a town hospital, where discipline would not allow him to get drunk or climb trees. For the 'Powers' had reasoned thus: To climb trees is bad; to get drunk is bad; but to do both puts on us too much responsibility; he must go! They had, in fact, been scared. And so he passed away to a room under the roof of a hospital in the big town miles away—la boîte indeed!—where for liberty he must use a courtyard without trees, and but little tobacco came to his cheek; and there he eats his heart out to this day, perhaps. But some say he had no heart—only the love of drink, and climbing. Yet, on that last evening, to one who was paying him for a little net, he blurted out: 'Some day I will tell you something—not now—in a year's time. Vous êtes le seul—!' What did he mean by that, if he had no heart to eat?... The night after he had gone, a little black dog strayed up, and among the trees barked and barked at some portent or phantom. 'Ah! the camel! Ah! the pig! I had him on my back all night!' Grandpère Poirot said next morning. That was the very last of Flotsam....

And now to Jetsam! It was on the day but one after Roche left that Gray was reported missing. For some time past he had been getting stronger, clearer in speech. They began to say of him: 'It's wonderful—the improvement since he came—wonderful!' His salvation also seemed in sight. But from the words 'He's rather a dear!' all recoiled, for as he grew stronger he became more stubborn and more irritable—'cunning egoist' that he was! According to the men, he was beginning to show himself in his true colours. He had threatened to knife any one who played a joke on him—the arrogant civilian! On the day that he was missing it appears that after the midday meal he had asked for a 'café natur' and for some reason had been refused. Before his absence was noted it was night already, clear and dark; all day something as of Spring had stirred in the air. The Corporal and a 'Power' set forth down the wooded hill into the town, to scour the cafés and hang over the swift, shallow river, to see if by any chance Gray had been overtaken by another paralytic stroke and was down there on the dark sand. The sleepy gendarmes too were warned and given his description. But the only news next morning was that he had been seen walking on the main road up the valley. Two days later he was found, twenty miles away, wandering towards Italy. 'Perdu' was his only explanation, but it was not believed, for now began that continual demand: 'Je voudrais aller à Lyon, voir mon oncle—travailler!' As the big cavalryman put it: 'He is bored here!' It was considered unreasonable, by soldiers who found themselves better off than in other hospitals; even the 'Powers' considered it ungrateful, almost. See what he had been like when he came—a mere trembling bag of bones, only too fearful of being sent away. And yet, who would not be bored, crouching all day long about the stoves, staunching his poor dribbling mouth, rolling his inevitable cigarette, or wandering down, lonely, to hang over the bridge parapet, having thoughts in his head and for ever unable to express them. His state was worse than dumbness, for the dumb have resigned hope of conversation. Gray would have liked to talk if it had not taken about five minutes to understand each thing he said—except the refrain which all knew by heart: 'Les Boches—ils vont en payer cher—les Boches!' The idea that he could work and earn his living was fantastic to those who watched him dressing himself, or sweeping the courtyard, pausing every few seconds to contemplate some invisible difficulty, or do over again what he had just not done. But with that new access of strength, or perhaps the open weather—as if Spring had come before its time—his fixed idea governed him completely; he began to threaten to kill himself if he could not go to work and see his uncle at Lyon; and every five days or so he had to be brought back from far up some hill road. The situation had become so ridiculous that the 'Powers' said in despair: 'Very well, my friend! Your uncle says he can't have you, and you can't earn your own living yet; but you shall go and see for yourself!' And go he did, a little solemn now that it had come to his point—in specially bought yellow boots—he refused black—and a specially bought overcoat with sleeves—he would have none of a pélerine, the arrogant civilian, no more than of a military capote. For a week the hospital knew him not. Deep winter set in two days before he went, and the whole land was wrapped in snow. The huge, disconsolate crows seemed all the life left in the valley, and poplar-trees against the rare blue sky were dowered with miraculous snow-blossoms, beautiful as any blossom of Spring. And still in the winter sun the town gossips sat on the bench under the wall, and the cross gleamed out, and the church bell, riding high in its whitened ironwork, tolled almost every day for the passing of some wintered soul, and long processions, very black in the white street, followed it, followed it—home. Then came a telegram from Gray's uncle: 'Impossible to keep Aristide (the name of the arrogant civilian), takes the evening train to-morrow. Albert Gray.' So Jetsam was coming back! What would he be like now that his fixed idea had failed him? Well! He came at midday; thinner, more clay-coloured in the face, with a bad cold; but he ate as heartily as ever, and at once asked to go to bed. At four o'clock a 'Power,' going up to see, found him sleeping like a child. He slept for twenty hours on end. No one liked to question him about his time away; all that he said—and bitterly—was: 'They wouldn't let me work!' But the second evening after his return there came a knock on the door of the little room where the 'Powers' were sitting after supper, and there stood Gray, long and shadowy, holding on to the screen, smoothing his jaw-bone with the other hand, turning eyes like a child's from face to face, while his helpless lips smiled. One of the 'Powers' said: 'What do you want, my friend?'

'Je voudrais aller à Paris, voir ma petite fille.'

'Yes, yes; after the war. Your petite fille is not in Paris, you know.'

'Non?' The smile was gone; it was seen too plainly that Gray was not as he had been. The access of vigour, stirring of new strength, 'improvement' had departed, but the beat of it, while there, must have broken him, as the beat of some too-strong engine shatters a frail frame. His 'improvement' had driven him to his own undoing. With the failure of his pilgrimage he had lost all hope, all 'egoism.'... It takes an eye, indeed, to tell salvation from damnation! He was truly Jetsam now—terribly thin and ill and sad; and coughing. Yet he kept the independence of his spirit. In that bitter cold, nothing could prevent him stripping to the waist to wash, nothing could keep him lying in bed, or kill his sense of the proprieties. He would not wear his overcoat—it was invalidish; he would not wear his new yellow boots and keep his feet dry, except on Sundays: 'Ils sont bons!' he would say. And before he would profane their goodness, his old worn-out shoes had to be reft from him. He would not admit that he was ill, that he was cold, that he was—anything. But at night, a 'Power' would be awakened by groans, and, hurrying to his room, find him huddled nose to knees, moaning. And now, every evening, as though craving escape from his own company, he would come to the little sitting-room, and stand with that deprecating smile, smoothing his jaw-bone, until some one said: 'Sit down, my friend, and have some coffee.' 'Merci, ma soeur—il est bon, il est bon!' and down he would sit, and roll a cigarette with his long fingers, tapering as any artist's, while his eyes fixed themselves intently on anything that moved. But soon they would stray off to another world, and he would say thickly, sullenly, fiercely: 'Les Boches—ils vont en payer cher—les Boches!' On the walls were some trophies from the war of 'seventy.' His eyes would gloat over them, and he would get up and finger a long pistol, or old papier-maché helmet. Never was a man who so lacked gêne—at home in any company; it inspired reverence, that independence of his, which had survived twenty months of imprisonment with those who, it is said, make their victims salute them—to such a depth has their civilisation reached. One night he tried to tell about the fright he had been given. The Boches—it seemed—had put him and two others against a wall, and shot those other two. Holding up two tapering fingers, he mumbled: 'Assassins—assassins! Ils vont en payer cher—les Boches!' But sometimes there was something almost beautiful in his face, as if his soul had rushed from behind his eyes, to answer some little kindness done to him, or greet some memory of the days before he was 'done for'—foutu, as he called it.

One day he admitted a pain about his heart; and time, too, for at moments he would look like death itself. His nurse, Corporal Mignan, had long left his 'deux phénomènes!' having drifted away on the tides of the system, till he should break down again and drag through the hospitals once more. Gray had a room to himself now; the arrogant civilian's groaning at night disturbed the others. Yet, if you asked him in the morning if he had slept well, he answered invariably, 'Oui—oui—toujours, toujours!' For, according to him, you see, he was still strong; and he would double his arm and tap his very little muscle, to show that he could work. But he did not believe it now, for one day a 'Power,' dusting the men's writing-room, saw a letter on the blotter, and with an ashamed eye read these words:—

'Cher Oncle,

J'ai eu la rage contre toi, mais c'est passé maintenant. Je veux seulement me reposer. Je ne peux pas me battre pour la France—j'ai voulu travailler pour elle; mais on ne m'a pas permi.

Votre neveu, qui t'embrasse de loin.'

Seulement me reposer—only to rest! Rest he will, soon, if eyes can speak. Pass, and leave for ever that ravished France for whom he wished to work—pass, without having seen again his petite fille. No more in the corridor above the stove, no more in the little dining-room or the avenue of pines will be seen his long, noiseless, lonely figure, or be heard his thick stumbling cry:

'Les Boches—ils vont en payer cher—les Boches!'

CHAPTER IV

THE BRIGHT SIDE

A little Englishwoman, married to a German, had dwelt with him eighteen years in humble happiness and the district of Putney, where her husband worked in the finer kinds of leather. He was a harmless, busy little man with the gift for turning his hand to anything which is bred into the peasants of the Black Forest, who on their upland farms make all the necessaries of daily life—their coarse linen from home-grown flax, their leather gear from the hides of their beasts, their clothes from the wool thereof, their furniture from the pine logs of the Forest, their bread from home-grown flour milled in simple fashion and baked in the home-made ovens, their cheese from the milk of their own goats. Why he had come to England he probably did not remember—it was so long ago; but he would still know why he had married Dora, the daughter of the Putney carpenter, she being, as it were, salt of the earth: one of those Cockney women, deeply sensitive beneath a well-nigh impermeable mask of humour and philosophy, who quite unselfconsciously are always doing things for others. In their little grey Putney house they had dwelt those eighteen years, without perhaps ever having had time to move, though they had often had the intention of doing so for the sake of the children, of whom they had three, a boy and two girls. Mrs. Gerhardt—she shall be called, for her husband had a very German name, and there is more in a name than Shakespeare dreamed of—Mrs. Gerhardt was a little woman with large hazel eyes and dark crinkled hair in which there were already a few threads of grey when the war broke out. Her boy David, the eldest, was fourteen at that date, and her girls, Minnie and Violet, were eight and five, rather pretty children, especially the little one. Gerhardt, perhaps because he was so handy, had never risen. His firm regarded him as indispensable and paid him fair wages, but he had no "push," having the craftsman's temperament, and employing his spare time in little neat jobs for his house and his neighbours, which brought him no return. They made their way, therefore, without that provision for the future which necessitates the employment of one's time for one's own ends. But they were happy, and had no enemies; and each year saw some mild improvements in their studiously clean house and tiny back garden. Mrs. Gerhardt, who was cook, seamstress, washerwoman, besides being wife and mother, was almost notorious in that street of semi-detached houses for being at the disposal of any one in sickness or trouble. She was not strong in body, for things had gone wrong when she bore her first, but her spirit had that peculiar power of seeing things as they were, and yet refusing to be dismayed, which so embarrasses Fate. She saw her husband's defects clearly, and his good qualities no less distinctly—they never quarrelled. She gauged her children's characters too, with an admirable precision, which left, however, loopholes of wonder as to what they would become.

The outbreak of the war found them on the point of going to Margate for Bank Holiday, an almost unparalleled event; so that the importance of the world catastrophe was brought home to them with a vividness which would otherwise have been absent from folks so simple, domestic, and far-removed from that atmosphere in which the egg of war is hatched. Over the origin and merits of the struggle, beyond saying to each other several times that it was a dreadful thing, Mr. and Mrs. Gerhardt held but one little conversation, lying in their iron bed with an immortal brown eiderdown patterned with red wriggles over them. They agreed that it was a cruel, wicked thing to invade "that little Belgium," and there left a matter which seemed to them a mysterious and insane perversion of all they had hitherto been accustomed to think of as life. Reading their papers—a daily and a weekly, in which they had as much implicit faith as a million other readers—they were soon duly horrified by the reports therein of "Hun" atrocities; so horrified that they would express their condemnation of the Kaiser and his militarism as freely as if they had been British subjects. It was therefore with an uneasy surprise that they began to find these papers talking of "the Huns at large in our midst," of "spies," and the national danger of "nourishing such vipers." They were deeply conscious of not being "vipers," and such sayings began to awaken in both their breasts a humble sense of injustice as it were. This was more acute in the breast of little Mrs. Gerhardt, because, of course, the shafts were directed not at her but at her husband. She knew her husband so well, knew him incapable of anything but homely, kindly busyness, and that he should be lumped into the category of "Huns" and "spies" and tarred with the brush of mass hatred amazed and stirred her indignation, or would have, if her Cockney temperament had allowed her to take it very seriously. As for Gerhardt, he became extremely silent, so that it was ever more and more difficult to tell what he was feeling. The patriotism of the newspapers took a considerable time to affect the charity of the citizens of Putney, and so long as no neighbour showed signs of thinking that little Gerhardt was a monster and a spy it was fairly easy for Mrs. Gerhardt to sleep at night, and to read her papers with the feeling that the remarks in them were not really intended for Gerhardt and herself. But she noticed that her man had given up reading them, and would push them away from his eyes if, in the tiny sitting-room with the heavily-flowered walls, they happened to rest beside him. He had perhaps a closer sense of impending Fate than she. The boy, David, went to his first work, and the girls to their school, and so things dragged on through that first long war winter and spring. Mrs. Gerhardt, in the intervals of doing everything, knitted socks for "our poor cold boys in the trenches," but Gerhardt no longer sought out little jobs to do in the houses of his neighbours. Mrs. Gerhardt thought that he "fancied" they would not like it. It was early in that spring that she took a deaf aunt to live with them, the wife of her mother's brother, no blood-relation, but the poor woman had nowhere else to go; so David was put to sleep on the horsehair sofa in the sitting-room because she "couldn't refuse the poor thing." And then, of an April afternoon, while she was washing the household sheets, her neighbour, Mrs. Clirehugh, a little spare woman all eyes, cheekbones, hair, and decision, came in breathless and burst out:

"Oh! Mrs. Gerhardt, 'ave you 'eard? They've sunk the Loositania! Has I said to Will: Isn't it horful?"

Mrs. Gerhardt, with her round arms dripping soap-suds, answered: "What a dreadful thing! The poor drowning people! Dear! Oh dear!"

"Oh! Those Huns! I'd shoot the lot, I would!"

"They are wicked!" Mrs. Gerhardt echoed: "That was a dreadful thing to do!"

But it was not till Gerhardt came in at five o'clock, white as a sheet, that she perceived how this dreadful catastrophe affected them.

"I have been called a German," were the first words he uttered; "Dollee, I have been called a German."

"Well, so you are, my dear," said Mrs. Gerhardt.

"You do not see," he answered, with a heat and agitation which surprised her. "I tell you this Lusitania will finish our business. They will have me. They will take me away from you all. Already the papers have: 'Intern all the Huns.'" He sat down at the kitchen table and buried his face in hands still grimy from his leather work. Mrs. Gerhardt stood beside him, her eyes unnaturally big.

"But Max," she said, "what has it to do with you? You couldn't help it. Max!"

Gerhardt looked up, his white face, broad in the brow and tapering to a thin chin, seemed all distraught.

"What do they care for that? Is my name Max Gerhardt? What do they care if I hate the war? I am a German. That's enough. You will see."

"Oh!" murmured Mrs. Gerhardt, "they won't be so unjust."

Gerhardt reached up and caught her chin in his hand, and for a moment those two pairs of eyes gazed, straining, into each other. Then he said:

"I don't want to be taken, Dollee. What shall I do away from you and the children? I don't want to be taken, Dollee."

Mrs. Gerhardt, with a feeling of terror and a cheerful smile, answered:

"You mustn't go fancyin' things, Max. I'll make you a nice cup of tea. Cheer up, old man! Look on the bright side!"

But Gerhardt lapsed into the silence which of late she had begun to dread.

That night some shop windows were broken, some German names effaced. The Gerhardts had no shop, no name painted up, and they escaped. In Press and Parliament the cry against "the Huns in our midst" rose with a fresh fury; but for the Gerhardts the face of Fate was withdrawn. Gerhardt went to his work as usual, and their laborious and quiet existence remained undisturbed; nor could Mrs. Gerhardt tell whether her man's ever-deepening silence was due to his "fancying things" or to the demeanour of his neighbours and fellow workmen. One would have said that he, like the derelict aunt, was deaf, so difficult to converse with had he become. His length of sojourn in England and his value to his employers, for he had real skill, had saved him for the time being; but, behind the screen, Fate twitched her grinning chaps.

Not till the howl which followed some air raids in 1916 did they take off Gerhardt, with a variety of other elderly men, whose crime it was to have been born in Germany. They did it suddenly, and perhaps it was as well, for a prolonged sight of his silent misery must have upset his family till they would have been unable to look on that bright side of things which Mrs. Gerhardt had, as it were, always up her sleeve. When, in charge of a big and sympathetic constable, he was gone, taking all she could hurriedly get together for him, she hastened to the police station. They were friendly to her there: She must cheer up, Missis, 'e'd be all right, she needn't worry. Ah! she could go down to the 'Ome Office, if she liked, and see what could be done. But they 'eld out no 'ope! Mrs. Gerhardt waited till the morrow, having the little Violet in bed with her, and crying quietly into her pillow; then, putting on her Sunday best she went down to a building in Whitehall, larger than any she had ever entered. Two hours she waited, sitting unobtrusive, with big anxious eyes, and a line between her brows. At intervals of half an hour she would get up and ask the messenger cheerfully: "I 'ope they haven't forgotten me, sir. Perhaps you'd see to it." And because she was cheerful the messenger took her under his protection, and answered: "All right, Missis. They're very busy, but I'll wangle you in some'ow."

When at length she was wangled into the presence of a grave gentleman in eye-glasses, realisation of the utter importance of this moment overcame her so that she could not speak. "Oh! dear"—she thought, while her heart fluttered like a bird—"he'll never understand; I'll never be able to make him." She saw her husband buried under the leaves of despair; she saw her children getting too little food, the deaf aunt, now bedridden, neglected in the new pressure of work that must fall on the only breadwinner left. And, choking a little, she said:

"I'm sure I'm very sorry to take up your time, sir; but my 'usband's been taken to the Palace; and we've been married over twenty years, and he's been in England twenty-five; and he's a very good man and a good workman; and I thought perhaps they didn't understand that; and we've got three children and a relation that's bedridden. And of course, we understand that the Germans have been very wicked; Gerhardt always said that himself. And it isn't as if he was a spy; so I thought if you could do something for us, sir, I being English myself."

The gentleman, looking past her at the wall, answered wearily:

"Gerhardt—I'll look into it. We have to do very hard things, Mrs. Gerhardt."

Little Mrs. Gerhardt, with big eyes almost starting out of her head, for she was no fool, and perceived that this was the end, said eagerly:

"Of course I know that there's a big outcry, and the papers are askin' for it; but the people in our street don't mind 'im, sir. He's always done little things for them; so I thought perhaps you might make an exception in his case."

She noticed that the gentleman's lips tightened at the word outcry, and that he was looking at her now.

"His case was before the Committee no doubt; but I'll inquire. Good-morning."

Mrs. Gerhardt, accustomed to not being troublesome, rose; a tear rolled down her cheek and was arrested by her smile.

"Thank you, sir, I'm sure. Good-morning, sir."

And she went out. Meeting the messenger in the corridor, and hearing his: "Well, Missis?" she answered: "I don't know. I must look on the bright side. Good-bye, and thank you for your trouble." And she turned away feeling as if she had been beaten all over.

The bright side on which she looked did not include the return to her of little Gerhardt, who was duly detained for the safety of the country. Obedient to economy, and with a dim sense that her favourite papers were in some way responsible for this, she ceased to take them in, and took in sewing instead. It had become necessary to do so, for the allowance she received from the government was about a quarter of Gerhardt's weekly earnings. In spite of its inadequacy it was something, and she felt she must be grateful. But, curiously enough, she could not forget that she was English, and it seemed strange to her that, in addition to the grief caused by separation from her husband from whom she had never been parted not even for a night, she should now be compelled to work twice as hard and eat half as much because that husband had paid her country the compliment of preferring it to his own. But, after all, many other people had much worse trouble to grieve over, so she looked on the bright side of all this, especially on those days once a week when alone, or accompanied by the little Violet, she visited that Palace where she had read in her favourite journals to her great comfort that her husband was treated like a prince. Since he had no money he was in what they called "the battalion," and their meetings were held in the bazaar, where things which "the princes" made were exposed for sale. Here Mr. and Mrs. Gerhardt would stand in front of some doll, some blotting-book, calendar, or walking-stick, which had been fashioned by one of "the princes." There they would hold each others' hands and try to imagine themselves unsurrounded by other men and wives, while the little Violet would stray and return to embrace her father's leg spasmodically. Standing there, Mrs. Gerhardt would look on the bright side, and explain to Gerhardt how well everything was going, and he mustn't fret about them, and how kind the police were, and how auntie asked after him, and Minnie would get a prize; and how he oughtn't to mope, but eat his food, and look on the bright side. And Gerhardt would smile the smile which went into her heart just like a sword, and say:

"All right, Dollee. I'm getting on fine." Then, when the whistle blew and he had kissed little Violet, they would be quite silent, looking at each other. And she would say in a voice so matter-of-fact that it could have deceived no one:

"Well, I must go now. Good-bye, old man!"

And he would say:

"Good-bye, Dollee. Kiss me."

They would kiss, and holding little Violet's hand very hard she would hurry away in the crowd, taking care not to look back for fear she might suddenly lose sight of the bright side. But as the months went on, became a year, eighteen months, two years, and still she went weekly to see her "prince" in his Palace, that visit became for her the hardest experience of all her hard week's doings. For she was a realist, as well as a heroine, and she could see the lines of despair not only in her man's heart but in his face. For a long time he had not said: "I'm getting on fine, Dollee." His face had a beaten look, his figure had wasted, he complained of his head.

"It's so noisy," he would say constantly; "oh! it's so noisy—never a quiet moment—never alone—never—never—never—never. And not enough to eat; it's all reduced now, Dollee."

She learned to smuggle food into his hands, but it was very little, for they had not enough at home either, with the price of living ever going up and her depleted income ever stationary. They had—her "man" told her—made a fuss in the papers about their being fed like turkeycocks, while the "Huns" were sinking the ships. Gerhardt, always a spare little man, had lost eighteen pounds. She, naturally well covered, was getting thin herself, but that she did not notice, too busy all day long, and too occupied in thinking of her "man." To watch him week by week, more hopeless, as the months dragged on, was an acute torture, to disguise which was torture even more acute. She had long seen that there was no bright side, but if she admitted that she knew she would go down; so she did not. And she carefully kept from Gerhardt such matters as David's overgrowing his strength, because she could not feed him properly; the completely bedridden nature of auntie; and worse than these, the growing coldness and unkindness of her neighbours. Perhaps they did not mean to be unkind, perhaps they did, for it was not in their nature to withstand the pressure of mass sentiment, the continual personal discomfort of having to stand in queues, the fear of air raids, the cumulative indignation caused by stories of atrocities true and untrue. In spite of her record of kindliness towards them she became tarred with the brush at last, for her nerves had given way once or twice, and she had said it was a shame to keep her man like that, gettin' iller and iller, who had never done a thing. Even her reasonableness—and she was very reasonable—succumbed to the strain of that weekly sight of him, till she could no longer allow for the difficulties which Mrs. Clirehugh assured her the Government had to deal with. Then one day she used the words "fair play," and at once it became current that she had "German sympathies." From that time on she was somewhat doomed. Those who had received kindnesses from her were foremost in showing her coldness, being wounded in their self-esteem. To have received little benefits, such as being nursed when they were sick, from one who had "German sympathies" was too much for the pride which is in every human being, however humble an inhabitant of Putney. Mrs. Gerhardt's Cockney spirit could support this for herself, but she could not bear it for her children. David came home with a black eye, and would not say why he had got it. Minnie missed her prize at school, though she had clearly won it. That was just after the last German offensive began; but Mrs. Gerhardt refused to see that this was any reason. Little Violet twice put the heart-rending question to her: "Aren't I English, Mummy?"

She was answered: "Yes, my dear, of course."

But the child obviously remained unconvinced in her troubled mind.

And then they took David for the British army. It was that which so upset the applecart in Mrs. Gerhardt that she broke out to her last friend, Mrs. Clirehugh:

"I do think it's hard, Eliza. They take his father and keep him there for a dangerous Hun year after year like that; and then they take his boy for the army to fight against him. And how I'm to get on without him I don't know."

Little Mrs. Clirehugh, who was Scotch, with a Gloucestershire accent, replied:

"Well, we've got to beat them. They're such a wicked lot. I daresay it's 'ard on you, but we've got to beat them."

"But we never did nothing," cried Mrs. Gerhardt; "it isn't us that's wicked. We never wanted the war; it's nothing but ruin to him. They did ought to let me have my man, or my boy, one or the other."

"You should 'ave some feeling for the Government, Dora; they 'ave to do 'ard things."

Mrs. Gerhardt, with a quivering face, had looked at her friend.

"I have," she said at last in a tone which implanted in Mrs. Clirehugh's heart the feeling that Dora was "bitter."

She could not forget it; and she would flaunt her head at any mention of her former friend. It was a blow to Mrs. Gerhardt, who had now no friends, except the deaf and bedridden aunt, to whom all things were the same, war or no war, Germans or no Germans, so long as she was fed.

About then it was that the tide turned, and the Germans began to know defeat. Even Mrs. Gerhardt, who read the papers no longer, learned it daily, and her heart relaxed; that bright side began to reappear a little. She felt they could not feel so hardly towards her "man" now as when they were all in fear; and perhaps the war would be over before her boy went out. But Gerhardt puzzled her. He did not brighten up. The iron seemed to have entered his soul too deeply. And one day, in the bazaar, passing an open doorway, Mrs. Gerhardt had a glimpse of why. There, stretching before her astonished eyes, was a great, as it were, encampment of brown blankets, slung and looped up anyhow, dividing from each other countless sordid beds, which were almost touching, and a whiff of huddled humanity came out to her keen nostrils, and a hum of sound to her ears. So that was where her man had dwelt these thirty months, in that dirty, crowded, noisy place, with dirty-looking men, such as those she could see lying on the beds, or crouching by the side of them, over their work. He had kept neat somehow, at least on the days when she came to see him—but that was where he lived! Alone again (for she no longer brought the little Violet to see her German father), she grieved all the way home. Whatever happened to him now, even if she got him back, she knew he would never quite get over it.

And then came the morning when she came out of her door like the other inhabitants of Putney, at sound of the maroons, thinking it was an air raid; and, catching the smile on the toothless mouth of one of her old neighbours, hearing the cheers of the boys in the school round the corner, knew that it was Peace. Her heart overflowed then, and, withdrawing hastily, she sat down on a shiny chair in her little empty parlour. Her face crumpled suddenly, the tears came welling forth; she cried and cried, alone in the little cold room. She cried from relief and utter thankfulness. It was over—over at last! The long waiting—the long misery—the yearning for her "man"—the grieving for all those poor boys in the mud, and the dreadful shell holes, and the fighting, the growing terror of anxiety for her own boy—over, all over! Now they would let Max out, now David would come back from the army; and people would not be unkind and spiteful to her and the children any more!

For all she was a Cockney, hers was a simple soul, associating Peace with Good-will. Drying her tears, she stood up, and in the little cheap mirror above the empty grate looked at her face. It was lined, and she was grey; for more than two years her man had not seen her without her hat. What ever would he say? And she rubbed and rubbed her cheeks, trying to smooth them out. Then her conscience smote her, and she ran upstairs to the back bedroom, where the deaf aunt lay. Taking up the little amateur ear trumpet which Gerhardt himself had made for "auntie," before he was taken away, she bawled into it:

"Peace, Auntie; it's Peace! Think of that. It's Peace!"

"What's that?" answered the deaf woman.

"It's Peace, Auntie, Peace."

The deaf lady roused herself a little, and some meaning came into the lack-lustre black eyes of her long, leathery face. "You don't say," she said in her wooden voice, "I'm so hungry, Dolly, isn't it time for my dinner?"

"I was just goin' to get it, dearie," replied Mrs. Gerhardt, and hurried back downstairs with her brain teeming, to make the deaf woman's bowl of bread, pepper, salt, and onions.

All that day and the next and the next she saw the bright side of things with almost dazzling clearness, waiting to visit her "prince" in his Palace. She found him in a strange and pitiful state of nerves. The news had produced too intense and varied emotions among those crowded thousands of men buried away from normal life so long. She spent all her hour and a half trying desperately to make him see the bright side, but he was too full of fears and doubts, and she went away smiling, but utterly exhausted. Slowly in the weeks which followed she learned that nothing was changed. In the fond hope that Gerhardt might be home now any day, she was taking care that his slippers and some clothes of David's were ready for him, and the hip bath handy for him to have a lovely hot wash. She had even bought a bottle of beer and some of his favourite pickle, saving the price out of her own food, and was taking in the paper again, letting bygones be bygones. But he did not come. And soon the paper informed her that the English prisoners were returning—many in wretched state, poor things, so that her heart bled for them, and made her fiercely angry with the cruel men who had treated them so; but it informed her too, that if the paper had its way no "Huns" would be tolerated in this country for the future. "Send them all back!" were the words it used. She did not realise at first that this applied to Gerhardt; but when she did, she dropped the journal as if it had been a living coal of fire. Not let him come back to his home, and family, not let him stay, after all they'd done to him, and he never did anything to them! Not let him stay, but send him out to that dreadful country, which he had almost forgotten in these thirty years, and he with an English wife and children! In this new terror of utter dislocation the bright side so slipped from her that she was obliged to go out into the back garden in the dark, where a sou'-westerly wind was driving the rain. There, lifting her eyes to the evening sky she uttered a little moan. It couldn't be true; and yet what they said in her paper had always turned out true, like the taking of Gerhardt away, and the reduction of his food. And the face of the gentleman in the building at Whitehall came before her out of the long past, with his lips tightening, and his words: "We have to do very hard things, Mrs. Gerhardt." Why had they to do them? Her man had never done no harm to no one! A flood, bitter as sea water, surged in her, and seemed to choke her very being. Those gentlemen in the papers—why should they go on like that? Had they no hearts, no eyes to see the misery they brought to humble folk? "I wish them nothing worse than what they've brought to him and me," she thought wildly: "nothing worse!"

The rain beat on her face, wetted her grey hair, cooled her eyeballs. "I mustn't be spiteful," she thought; and bending down in the dark she touched the glass of the tiny conservatory built against the warm kitchen wall, and heated by the cunning little hot-water pipe her man had put there in his old handy days. Under it were one little monthly rose, which still had blossoms, and some straggly small chrysanthemums. She had been keeping them for the feast when he came home; but if he wasn't to come, what should she do? She raised herself. Above the wet roofs sky-rack was passing wild and dark, but in a little cleared space one or two stars shone the brighter for the blackness below. "I must look on the bright side," she thought, "or I can't bear myself." And she went in to cook the porridge for the evening meal.

The winter passed for her in the most dreadful anxiety. "Repatriate the Huns!" That cry continued to spurt up in her paper like a terrible face seen in some recurrent nightmare; and each week that she went to visit Gerhardt brought solid confirmation to her terror. He was taking it hard, so that sometimes she was afraid that "something" was happening in him. This was the utmost she went towards defining what doctors might have diagnosed as incipient softening of the brain. He seemed to dread the prospect of being sent to his native country.

"I couldn't stick it, Dollee," he would say. "What should I do—whatever should I do? I haven't a friend. I haven't a spot to go to. I should be lost. I'm afraid, Dollee. How could you come out there, you and the children? I couldn't make a living for you. I couldn't make one for myself now."

And she would say: "Cheer up, old man. Look on the bright side. Think of the others." For, though those others were not precisely the bright side, the mental picture of their sufferings, all those poor "princes" and their families, somehow helped her to bear her own. But he shook his head:

"No; I should never see you again."

"I'd follow you," she answered. "Never fear, Max, we'd work in the fields—me and the children. We'd get on somehow. Bear up, my dearie. It'll soon be over now. I'll stick to you, Max, never you fear. But they won't send you, they never will."

And then, like a lump of ice pressed on her breast, came the thought: "But if they do! Auntie! My boy! My girls! However shall I manage if they do!"

Then long lists began to appear, and in great batches men were shovelled wholesale back to the country whose speech some of them had well-nigh forgotten. Little Gerhardt's name had not appeared yet. The lists were hung up the day after Mrs. Gerhardt's weekly visit, but she urged him if his name did appear to appeal against repatriation. It was with the greatest difficulty that she roused in him the energy to promise. "Look on the bright side, Max," she implored him. "You've got a son in the British army; they'll never send you. They wouldn't be so cruel. Never say die, old man."

His name appeared but was taken out, and the matter hung again in awful suspense, while the evil face of the recurrent nightmare confronted Mrs. Gerhardt out of her favourite journal. She read that journal again, because, so far as in her gentle spirit lay, she hated it. It was slowly killing her man, and all her chance of future happiness; she hated it, and read it every morning. To the monthly rose and straggly little brown-red chrysanthemums in the tiny hothouse there had succeeded spring flowers—a few hardy January snowdrops, and one by one blue scillas, and the little pale daffodils called "angels' tears."

Peace tarried, but the flowers came up long before their time in their tiny hothouse against the kitchen flue. And then one wonderful day there came to Mrs. Gerhardt a strange letter, announcing that Gerhardt was coming home. He would not be sent to Germany—he was coming home! To-day, that very day—any moment he might be with her. When she received it, who had long received no letters save the weekly letters of her boy still in the army, she was spreading margarine on auntie's bread for breakfast, and, moved beyond all control, she spread it thick, wickedly, wastefully thick, then dropped the knife, sobbed, laughed, clasped her hands on her breast, and without rhyme or reason, began singing: "Hark! the herald angels sing." The girls had gone to school already, auntie in the room above could not hear her, no one heard her, nor saw her drop suddenly into the wooden chair, and, with her bare arms stretched out one on either side of the plate of bread and margarine, cry her heart out against the clean white table. Coming home, coming home, coming home! The bright side! The little white stars!

It was a quarter of an hour before she could trust herself to answer the knocking on the floor, which meant that "auntie" was missing her breakfast. Hastily she made the tea and went up with it and the bread and margarine. The woman's dim long face gleamed greedily when she saw how thick the margarine was spread; but little Mrs. Gerhardt said no word of the reason for that feast. She just watched her only friend eating it, while a little moisture still trickled out from her big eyes on to her flushed cheeks, and the words still hummed in her brain:

"Peace on earth and mercy mild, Jesus Christ a little child."

Then, still speaking no word, she ran out and put clean sheets on her and her man's bed. She was on wires, she could not keep still, and all the morning she polished, polished. About noon she went out into her garden, and from under the glass plucked every flower that grew there—snowdrops, scillas, "angels' tears," quite two dozen blossoms. She brought them into the little parlour and opened its window wide. The sun was shining, and fell on the flowers strewn on the table, ready to be made into the nosegay of triumphant happiness. While she stood fingering them, delicately breaking half an inch off their stalks so that they should last the longer in water, she became conscious of someone on the pavement outside the window, and looking up saw Mrs. Clirehugh. The past, the sense of having been deserted by her friends, left her, and she called out:

"Come in, Eliza; look at my flowers!"

Mrs. Clirehugh came in; she was in black, her cheekbones higher, her hair looser, her eyes bigger. Mrs. Gerhardt saw tears starting from those eyes, wetting those high cheekbones, and cried out:

"Why, what's the matter, dear?"

Mrs. Clirehugh choked. "My baby!"

Mrs. Gerhardt dropped an "angels' tear," and went up to her.

"Whatever's happened?" she cried.

"Dead!" replied Mrs. Clirehugh. "Dead o' the influenza. 'E's to be buried to-day. I can't—I can't—I can't—" Wild choking stopped her utterance. Mrs. Gerhardt put an arm round her and drew her head on to her shoulder.

"I can't—I can't—" sobbed Mrs. Clirehugh; "I can't find any flowers. It's seein' yours made me cry."

"There, there!" cried Mrs. Gerhardt. "Have them. I'm sure you're welcome, dearie. Have them—I'm so sorry!"

"I don't know," choked Mrs. Clirehugh, "I 'aven't deserved them." Mrs. Gerhardt gathered up the flowers.

"Take them," she said. "I couldn't think of it. Your poor little baby. Take them! There, there, he's spared a lot of trouble. You must look on the bright side, dearie."

Mrs. Clirehugh tossed up her head.

"You're an angel, that's what you are!" she said, and grasping the flowers she hurried out, a little black figure passing the window in the sunlight.

Mrs. Gerhardt stood above the emptied table, thinking: "Poor dear—I'm glad she had the flowers. It was a mercy I didn't call out that Max was coming!" And from the floor she picked up one "angels' tear" she had dropped, and set it in a glass of water, where the sunlight fell. She was still gazing at it, pale, slender, lonely in that coarse tumbler, when she heard a knock on the parlour door, and went to open it. There stood her man, with a large brown-paper parcel in his hand. He stood quite still, his head a little down, the face very grey. She cried out; "Max!" but the thought flashed through her: "He knocked on the door! It's his door—he knocked on the door!"

"Dollee?" he said, with a sort of question in his voice.

She threw her arms round him, drew him into the room, and shutting the door, looked hard into his face. Yes, it was his face, but in the eyes something wandered—lit up, went out, lit up.

"Dollee," he said again, and clutched her hand.

She strained him to her with a sob.

"I'm not well, Dollee," he murmured.

"No, of course not, my dearie man; but you'll soon be all right now—home again with me. Cheer up, cheer up!"

"I'm not well," he said again.

She caught the parcel out of his hand, and taking the "angels' tear" from the tumbler, fixed it in his coat.

"Here's a spring flower for you, Max; out of your own little hothouse. You're home again; home again, my dearie. Auntie's upstairs, and the girls'll be coming soon. And we'll have dinner."

"I'm not well, Dollee," he said.

Terrified by that reiteration, she drew him down on the little horsehair sofa, and sat on his knee. "You're home, Max, kiss me. There's my man!" and she rocked him to and fro against her, yearning yet fearing to look into his face and see that "something" wander there—light up, go out, light up. "Look, dearie," she said, "I've got some beer for you. You'd like a glass of beer?"

He made a motion of his lips, a sound that was like the ghost of a smack. It terrified her, so little life was there in it.

He clutched her close, and repeated feebly:

"Yes, all right in a day or two. They let me come—I'm not well, Dollee." He touched his head.

Straining him to her, rocking him, she murmured over and over again, like a cat purring to its kitten:

"It's all right, my dearie—soon be well—soon be well! We must look on the bright side—My man!"

CHAPTER V

"CAFARD"

The soldier Jean Liotard lay, face to the earth, by the bank of the river Drôme. He lay where the grass and trees ended, and between him and the shrivelled green current was much sandy foreshore, for summer was at height, and the snows had long finished melting and passing down. The burning sun had sucked up all moisture, the earth was parched, but to-day a cool breeze blew, willow and aspen leaves were fluttering and hissing as if millions of tiny kisses were being given up there; and a few swathes of white cloud were drawn, it seemed—not driven—along the blue. The soldier Jean Liotard had fixed his eyes on the ground, where was nothing to see but a few dry herbs. He had "cafard," for he was due to leave the hospital to-morrow and go up before the military authorities, for "prolongation." There he would answer perfunctory questions, and be told at once: Au dépôt; or have to lie naked before them that some "major" might prod his ribs, to find out whether his heart, displaced by shell-shock, had gone back sufficiently to normal position. He had received one "prolongation," and so, wherever his heart now was, he felt sure he would not get another. "Au dépôt" was the fate before him, fixed as that river flowing down to its death in the sea. He had "cafard"—the little black beetle in the brain, which gnaws and eats and destroys all hope and heaven in a man. It had been working at him all last week, and now he was at a monstrous depth of evil and despair. To begin again the cursed barrack-round, the driven life, until in a month perhaps, packed like bleating sheep, in the troop-train, he made that journey to the fighting line again—"À la hachette—à la hachette!"

He had stripped off his red flannel jacket, and lay with shirt opened to the waist, to get the breeze against his heart. In his brown good-looking face the hazel eyes, which in these three God-deserted years had acquired a sort of startled gloom, stared out like a dog's, rather prominent, seeing only the thoughts within him—thoughts and images swirling round and round in a dark whirlpool, drawing his whole being deeper and deeper. He was unconscious of all the summer hum and rustle—the cooing of the dove up in that willow tree, the winged enamelled fairies floating past, the chirr of the cicadas, that little brown lizard among the pebbles, almost within reach, seeming to listen to the beating of summer's heart so motionless it lay; unconscious, as though in verity he were again deep in some stifling trench, with German shells whining over him, and the smell of muck and blood making foetid the air. He was in the mood which curses God and dies; for he was devout—a Catholic, and still went to Mass. And God had betrayed the earth, and Jean Liotard. All the enormities he had seen in his two years at the front— the mouthless mangled faces, the human ribs whence rats would steal; the frenzied tortured horses, with leg or quarter rent away, still living; the rotted farms, the dazed and hopeless peasants; his innumerable suffering comrades; the desert of no-man's land; and all the thunder and moaning of war; and the reek and the freezing of war; and the driving—the callous perpetual driving, by some great Force which shovelled warm human hearts and bodies, warm human hopes and loves by the million into the furnace; and over all, dark sky without a break, without a gleam of blue, or lift anywhere—all this enclosed him, lying in the golden heat, so that not a glimmer of life or hope could get at him. Back into it all again! Back into it, he who had been through forty times the hell that the "majors" ever endured, five hundred times the hell ever glimpsed at by those députés, safe with their fat salaries, and their gabble about victory and the lost provinces, and the future of the world—the Canaille! Let them allow the soldiers, whose lives they spent like water—"les camarades" on both sides—poor devils who bled, and froze, and starved, and sweated—let them suffer these to make the peace! Ah! What a peace that would be—its first condition, all the sacred politicians and pressmen hanging in rows in every country; the mouth fighters, the pen fighters, the fighters with other men's blood! Those comfortable citizens would never rest till there was not a young man with whole limbs left in France! Had he not killed enough Boches, that they might leave him and his tired heart in peace? He thought of his first charge; of how queer and soft that Boche body felt when his bayonet went through; and another, and another. Ah! he had "joliment" done his duty that day! And something wrenched at his ribs. They were only Boches, but their wives and children, their mothers—faces questioning, faces pleading for them—pleading with whom? Ah! Not with him! Who was he that had taken those lives, and others since, but a poor devil without a life himself, without the right to breathe or move except to the orders of a Force which had no mind, which had no heart, had nothing but a blind will to go on, it knew not why. If only he survived—it was not possible—but if only he survived, and with his millions of comrades could come back and hold the reckoning! Some scare-the-crows then would waggle in the wind. The butterflies would perch on a few mouths empty at last; the flies enjoy a few silent tongues! Then slowly his fierce unreasoning rancour vanished into a mere awful pity for himself. Was a fellow never again to look at the sky, and the good soil, the fruit, the wheat, without this dreadful black cloud above him, never again make love among the trees, or saunter down a lighted boulevard, or sit before a café, never again attend Mass, without this black dog of disgust and dread sitting on his shoulders, riding him to death? Angels of pity! Was there never to be an end? One was going mad under it—yes, mad! And the face of his mother came before him, as he had seen her last, just three years ago, when he left his home in the now invaded country, to join his regiment—his mother who, with all his family, was in the power of the Boche. He had gone gaily, and she had stood like stone, her hand held over her eyes, in the sunlight, watching him while the train ran out. Usually the thought of the cursed Boches holding in their heavy hands all that was dear to him, was enough to sweep his soul to a clear, definite hate, which made all this nightmare of war seem natural, and even right; but now it was not enough—he had "cafard." He turned on his back. The sky above the mountains might have been black for all the joy its blue gave him. The butterflies, those drifting flakes of joy, passed unseen. He was thinking: No rest, no end, except by walking over bodies, dead, mangled bodies of poor devils like himself, poor hunted devils, who wanted nothing but never to lift a hand in combat again so long as they lived, who wanted—as he wanted— nothing but laughter and love and rest! Quelle vie! A carnival of leaping demonry! A dream— unutterably bad! "And when I go back to it all," he thought, "I shall go all shaven and smart, and wave my hand as if I were going to a wedding, as we all do. Vive la France! Ah! what mockery! Can't a poor devil have a dreamless sleep!" He closed his eyes, but the sun struck hot on them through the lids, and he turned over on his face again, and looked longingly at the river—they said it was deep in mid-stream; it still ran fast there! What was that down by the water? Was he really mad? And he uttered a queer laugh. There was his black dog—the black dog off his shoulders, the black dog which rode him, yea, which had become his very self, just going to wade in! And he called out:

"Hé! le copain!" It was not his dog, for it stopped drinking, tucked its tail in, and cowered at the sound of his voice. Then it came from the water, and sat down on its base among the stones, and looked at him. A real dog was it? What a guy! What a thin wretch of a little black dog! It sat and stared—a mongrel who might once have been pretty. It stared at Jean Liotard with the pathetic gaze of a dog so thin and hungry that it earnestly desires to go to men and get fed once more, but has been so kicked and beaten that it dare not. It seemed held in suspense by the equal overmastering impulses, fear and hunger. And Jean Liotard stared back. The lost, as it were despairing look of the dog began to penetrate his brain. He held out his hand and said: "Viens!" But at the sound the little dog only squirmed away a few paces, then again sat down, and resumed its stare. Again Jean Liotard uttered that queer laugh. If the good God were to hold out his hand and say to him: "Viens!" he would do exactly as that little beast; he would not come, not he! What was he too but a starved and beaten dog—a driven wretch, kicked to hell! And again, as if experimenting with himself, he held out his hand and said: "Viens!" and again the beast squirmed a little further away, and again sat down and stared. Jean Liotard lost patience. His head drooped till his forehead touched the ground. He smelt the parched herbs, and a faint sensation of comfort stole through his nerves. He lay unmoving, trying to fancy himself dead and out of it all. The hum of summer, the smell of grasses, the caress of the breeze going over! He pressed the palms of his outstretched hands on the warm soil, as one might on a woman's breast. If only it were really death, how much better than life in this butcher's shop! But death, his death was waiting for him away over there, under the moaning shells, under the whining bullets, at the end of a steel prong—a mangled, foetid death. Death—his death, had no sweet scent, and no caress—save the kisses of rats and crows. Life and Death what were they? Nothing but the preying of creatures the one on the other—nothing but that; and love, the blind instinct which made these birds and beasts of prey. Bon sang de bon sang! The Christ hid his head finely nowadays! That cross up there on the mountain top, with the sun gleaming on it—they had been right to put it up where no man lived, and not even a dog roamed, to be pitied! "Fairy tales, fairy tales," he thought; "those who drive and those who are driven, those who eat and those who are eaten—we are all poor devils together. There is no pity, no God!" And the flies drummed their wings above him. And the sun, boring into his spine through his thin shirt, made him reach for his jacket. There was the little dog, still, sitting on its base, twenty yards away. It cowered and dropped its ears when he moved; and he thought "Poor beast! Someone has been doing the devil's work on you, not badly!" There were some biscuits in the pocket of his jacket, and he held one out. The dog shivered, and its thin pink tongue lolled out, panting with desire, and fear. Jean Liotard tossed the biscuit gently about half way. The dog cowered back a step or two, crept forward three, and again squatted. Then very gradually it crept up to the biscuit, bolted it, and regained its distance. The soldier took out another. This time he threw it five paces only in front of him. Again the little beast cowered, slunk forward, seized the biscuit, devoured it; but this time it only recoiled a pace or two, and seemed, with panting mouth and faint wagging of the tail, to beg for more. Jean Liotard held a third biscuit as far out in front of him as he could, and waited. The creature crept forward and squatted just out of reach. There it sat, with saliva dripping from its mouth; seemingly it could not make up its mind to that awful venture. The soldier sat motionless; his outstretched hand began to tire; but he did not budge—he meant to conquer its fear. At last it snatched the biscuit. Jean Liotard instantly held out a fourth. That too was snatched, but at the fifth he was able to touch the dog. It cowered almost into the ground at touch of his fingers, and then lay, still trembling violently, while the soldier continued to stroke its head and ears. And suddenly his heart gave a twitter, the creature had licked his hand. He took out his last biscuit, broke it up, and fed the dog slowly with the bits, talking all the time; when the last crumb was gone he continued to murmur and crumple its ears softly. He had become aware of something happening within the dog—something in the nature of conversion, as if it were saying: "O my master, my new master—I worship, I love you!" The creature came gradually closer, quite close; then put up its sharp black nose and began to lick his face. Its little hot rough tongue licked and licked, and with each lick the soldier's heart relaxed, just as if the licks were being given there, and something licked away. He put his arms round the thin body, and hugged it, and still the creature went on feverishly licking at his face, and neck, and chest, as if trying to creep inside him. The sun poured down, the lizards rustled and whisked among the pebbles; the kissing never ceased up there among the willow and aspen leaves, and every kind of flying thing went past drumming its wings. There was no change in the summer afternoon. God might not be there, but Pity had come back; Jean Liotard no longer had "cafard." He put the little dog gently off his lap, got up, and stretched himself. "Voyons, mon brave, faut aller voir les copains! Tu es à moi." The little dog stood up on its hind legs, scratching with its forepaws at the soldier's thigh, as if trying to get at his face again; as if begging not to be left; and its tail waved feverishly, half in petition, half in rapture. The soldier caught the paws, set them down, and turned his face for home, making the noises that a man makes to his dog; and the little dog followed, close as he could get to those moving ankles, lifting his snout, and panting with anxiety and love.

CHAPTER VI

RECORDED

Just as the train was going out the compartment was stormed by a figure in khaki, with a rifle, a bad cold, a wife, a basket, a small bundle, and two babies. Setting his rifle down in the corner, he said:

"Didn't think we shud ever 'a caught it!"

His lean face was streaming with perspiration, and when he took off his overcoat there rose the sweetish sourish scent of a hot goatskin waistcoat. It reached below his waist, and would have kept cold out from a man standing in a blizzard, and he had been carrying a baby, a rifle, a bundle, a basket, and running, on a warmish day.

"Grand things, these," he said, and took it off. He also took off his cap, and sat down with the elder baby in a howling draught.

"Proper cold I've caught comin' over here," he added.

His wife, quite a girl, broad-faced, fresh-coloured, with small grey eyes and a wonderfully placid, comely face, on which a faint shadow seemed printed, sat beside him with the younger baby, a real hairless one, as could be seen when its white knitted cap slipped. The elder baby, perhaps two years old, began whimpering a little. He jigged it gently, and said:

"We 'ad a lot o' trouble wi' this one yesterday. The Doctor didn't think 'er fit to travel; but I got to see the old people down there, before I go back out across. Come over Sunday night—only got a week's leave. So here we are," and he laughed.

"What is your corps?" I asked.

"Engineers."

"Join since the war?"

He looked at me as if to say: What a question!

"Twelve years' service. Been everywhere—India, South Africa, Egypt. Come over to the front from Egypt."

"Where? Ypres?"

"Beg pardon? Wipers? No, Labassy."

"Rough time?"

He winked. "Proper rough time."

He looked straight at me, and his eyes—Celtic-grey, with a good deal of light in them—stared, wide and fixed, at things beyond me, as only do the eyes of those who have seen much death. There was a sort of burnt-gunpowder look about their rims and lashes, and a fixity that nothing could have stared down.

"The Kazer he says it'll all be over by April!" He laughed, abandoning the whole of him to enjoyment of that joke.

He was thin as a rail; his head with its thick brown hair was narrow, his face narrowish too. He had irregular ears, and no feature that could be called good, but his expression was utterly genuine and unconscious of itself. When he sat quiet his face would be held a little down, his eyes would be looking at something—or was it nothing?—far-off, in a kind of frowning dream. But if he glanced at his babies his rather thick mouth became all smiles, and he would make a remark to his wife about them. Once or twice she looked at him softly, but I could never catch him responding to that; his life was rather fuller than hers just now. Presently she took from him the elder baby which, whimpering again, was quieted at once by her broad placidity. The younger baby she passed to him; and, having secured it on his knee, he said:

"This one's a proper little gem; never makes a sound; she's a proper little gem. Never cude stand hearin' a baby cry." It certainly was an admirable baby, whether her little garments were lifted so that you saw portions of her—scarlet from being held too tight, whether the shawl was wrapped over her too much or too little, or her little knitted trousers seemed about to fall off. For both these babies were elegantly dressed, and so was the mother, with a small blue hat and a large-checked blouse over her broad bosom, and a blue skirt all crumbs and baby. It was pleasant to see that he had ceased to stream with perspiration now, and some one at the other end of the carriage having closed the window, he and the babies no longer sat in a howling draught—not that they had ever noticed it.

"Yes," he said suddenly, "proper rough time we 'ad of it at first. Terrible—yu cude 'ardly stick it. We Engineers 'ad the worst of it, tu. But must laugh, you know; if yu're goin' to cop it next minute—must laugh!" And he did. But his eyes didn't quite lose that stare.

"How did you feel the first day under fire?"

He closed one eye and shook his head.

"Not very grand—not very grand—not for two or three days. Soon get used to it, though. Only things I don't care about now are those Jack Johnsons. Long Toms out in South Africa—now Jack Johnsons—funny names—" and he went into a roar. Then leaning forward and, to make sure of one's attention, sawing the air with a hand that held perhaps the longest used handkerchief ever seen, "I seen 'em make a hole where you could 'ave put two 'underd and fifty horses. Don't think I shall ever get to like 'em. Yu don't take no notice o' rifle fire after a little—not a bit o' notice. I was out once with a sapper and two o' the Devons, fixin' up barbed wire—bullets strikin' everywhere just like rain. One o' the Devons, he was sittin' on a biscuit-tin, singin': 'The fields were white wi' daisies'—singing. All of a sudden he goes like this—" And giving a queer dull "sumph" of a sound, he jerked his body limp towards his knees—"Gone! Dig a hole, put 'im in. Your turn to-morrow, perhaps. Pals an' all. Yu get so as yu don't take no notice."

On the face of the broad, placid girl with the baby against her breast the shadow seemed printed a little deeper, but she did not wince. The tiny baby on his knees woke up and crowed faintly. He smiled.

"Since I been out there, I've often wished I was a little 'un again, like this. Well, I made up my mind when first I went for a soldier, that I'd like to 'ave a medal out of it some day. Now I'll get it, if they don't get me!" and he laughed again: "Ah! I've 'ad some good times, an' I've 'ad some bad times—"

"But never a time like this?"

"Yes, I reckon this has about put the top hat on it!" and he nodded his head above the baby's. "About put the top hat on! Oh! I've seen things—enough to make your 'eart bleed. I've seen a lot of them country people. Cruel it is! Women, old men, little children, 'armless people—enough to make your 'eart bleed. I used to think of the folk over 'ere. Don't think English women'd stand what the French and Belgian women do. Those poor women over there—wonderful they are. There yu'll see 'em sittin' outside their 'omes just a heap o' ruins—clingin' to 'em. Wonderful brave and patient—make your 'eart bleed to see 'em. Things I've seen! There's some proper brutes among the Germans—must be. Yu don't feel very kind to 'em when yu've seen what I've seen. We 'ave some games with 'em, though"—he laughed again: "Very nervous people, the Germans. If we stop firin' in our lines, up they send the star shells, rockets and all, to see what's goin' on—think we're goin' to attack—regular 'lumination o' fireworks—very nervous people. Then we send up some rockets on our side—just to 'ave some fun—proper display o' fireworks." He went off into a roar: "Must 'ave a bit o' fun, you know."

"Is it true they can't stand the bayonet?"

"Yes, that's right—they'll tell yu so themselves—very sensitive, nervous people."

And after that a silence fell. The elder babe was still fretful, and the mother's face had on it that most moving phenomenon of this world—the strange, selfless, utterly absorbed look, mouth just loosened, eyes off where we cannot follow, the whole being wrapped in warmth of her baby against her breast. And he, with the tiny placid baby, had gone off into another sort of dream, with his slightly frowning, far-away look. What was it all about?—nothing perhaps! A great quality, to be able to rest in vacancy.

He stirred and I offered him the paper, but he shook his head.

"Thank yu; don't care about lookin' at 'em. They don't know half what we do out there—from what I've seen of 'em since I come back, I don't seem to 'ave any use for 'em. The pictures, too—" He shrugged and shook his head. "We 'ave the real news, y'see. They don't keep nothin' from us. But we're not allowed to say. When we advance there'll be some lives lost, I tell yu!"

He nodded, thinking for a second perhaps of his own. "Can't be helped! Once we get 'em on the run, we shan't give 'em much time." Just then the baby on his knee woke up and directed on him the full brunt of its wide-open bright grey eyes. Its rosy cheeks were so broad and fat that its snub nose seemed but a button; its mouth, too tiny, one would think, for use, smiled. Seeing that smile he said:

"Well, what do yu want? Proper little gem, ain't yu!" And suddenly looking up at me, he added with a sort of bashful glee: "My old people'll go fair mad when they see me—go fair mad they will." He seemed to dwell on the thought, and I saw the wife give him a long soft smiling look. He added suddenly:

"I'll 'ave to travel back, though, Saturday—catch the six o'clock from Victoria, Sunday—to cross over there."

Very soon after that we arrived at where he changed, and putting on his goatskin, his cap, and overcoat, he got out behind his wife, carrying with the utmost care those queer companions, his baby and his rifle.

Where is he now? Alive, dead? Who knows?

CHAPTER VII

THE RECRUIT

Several times since that fateful Fourth of August he had said: "I sh'll 'ave to go."

And the farmer and his wife would look at him, he with a sort of amusement, she with a queer compassion in her heart, and one or the other would reply smiling: "That's all right, Tom, there's plenty Germans yet. Yu wait a bit."

His mother, too, who came daily from the lonely cottage in the little combe on the very edge of the big hill to work in the kitchen and farm dairy, would turn her dark taciturn head, with still plentiful black hair, towards his face which, for all its tan, was so weirdly reminiscent of a withered baby, pinkish and light-lashed, with forelock and fair hair thin and rumpled, and small blue eyes, and she would mutter:

"Don't yu never fret, boy. They'll come for 'ee fast enough when they want 'ee." No one, least of all perhaps his mother, could take quite seriously that little square short-footed man, born when she was just seventeen. Sure of work because he was first-rate with every kind of beast, he was yet not looked on as being quite 'all there.' He could neither read nor write, had scarcely ever been outside the parish, and then only in a shandrydan on a Club treat, and he knew no more of the world than the native of a small South Sea Island. His life from school age on had been passed year in, year out, from dawn till dark, with the cattle and their calves, the sheep, the horses and the wild moor ponies; except when hay or corn harvest, or any exceptionally exacting festival absorbed him for the moment. From shyness he never went into the bar of the Inn, and so had missed the greater part of village education. He could of course read no papers, a map was to him but a mystic mass of marks and colours; he had never seen the sea, never a ship; no water broader than the parish streams; until the war had never met anything more like a soldier than the constable of the neighbouring village. But he had once seen a Royal Marine in uniform. What sort of creatures these Germans were to him—who knows? They were cruel—he had grasped that. Something noxious, perhaps, like the adders whose backs he broke with his stick; something dangerous like the chained dog at Shapton Farm; or the big bull at Vannacombe. When the war first broke out, and they had called the younger blacksmith (a reservist and noted village marksman) back to his regiment, the little cowman had smiled and said: "Wait till regiment gets to front, Fred'll soon shoot 'em up."

But weeks and months went by, and it was always the Germans, the Germans; Fred had clearly not yet shot them up; and now one and now another went off from the village, and two from the farm itself; and the great Fred returned slightly injured for a few weeks' rest, and, full of whisky from morning till night, made the village ring; and finally went off again in a mood of manifest reluctance. All this weighed dumbly on the mind of the little cowman, the more heavily that because of his inarticulate shyness he could never talk that weight away, nor could anyone by talk relieve him, no premises of knowledge or vision being there. From sheer physical contagion he felt the grizzly menace in the air, and a sense of being left behind when others were going to meet that menace with their fists, as it were. There was something proud and sturdy in the little man, even in the look of him, for all that he was 'poor old Tom,' who brought a smile to the lips of all. He was passionate, too, if rubbed up the wrong way; but it needed the malevolence and ingenuity of human beings to annoy him—with his beasts he never lost his temper, so that they had perfect confidence in him. He resembled indeed herdsmen of the Alps, whom one may see in dumb communion with their creatures up in those high solitudes; for he too dwelt in a high solitude cut off from real fellowship with men and women by lack of knowledge, and by the supercilious pity in them. Living in such a remote world his talk—when he did say something—had ever the surprising quality attaching to the thoughts of those by whom the normal proportions of things are quite unknown. His short square figure, hatless and rarely coated in any weather, dotting from foot to foot, a bit of stick in one hand, and often a straw in the mouth—he did not smoke—was familiar in the yard where he turned the handle of the separator, or in the fields and cowsheds, from daybreak to dusk, save for the hours of dinner and tea, which he ate in the farm kitchen, making sparse and surprising comments. To his peculiar whistles and calls the cattle and calves, for all their rumination and stubborn shyness, were amazingly responsive. It was a pretty sight to see them pushing against each other round him—for, after all, he was as much the source of their persistence, especially through the scanty winter months, as a mother starling to her unfledged young.

When the Government issued their request to householders to return the names of those of military age ready to serve if called on, he heard of it, and stopped munching to say in his abrupt fashion: "I'll go—fight the Germans." But the farmer did not put him down, saying to his wife:

"Poor old Tom! 'Twidden be 'ardly fair—they'd be makin' game of 'un."

And his wife, her eyes shining with motherliness, answered: "Poor lad, he's not fit-like."

The months went on—winter passing to spring—and the slow decking of the trees and fields began with leaves and flowers, with butterflies and the songs of birds. How far the little cowman would notice such a thing as that no one could ever have said, devoid as he was of the vocabulary of beauty, but like all the world his heart must have felt warmer and lighter under his old waistcoat, and perhaps more than most hearts, for he could often be seen standing stock-still in the fields, his browning face turned to the sun.

Less and less he heard talk of Germans—dogged acceptance of the state of war having settled on that far countryside—the beggars were not beaten and killed off yet, but they would be in good time. It was unpleasant to think of them more than could be helped. Once in a way a youth went off and "listed,' but though the parish had given more perhaps than the average, a good few of military age still clung to life as they had known it. Then some bright spirit conceived the notion that a county regiment should march through the remoter districts to rouse them up.

The cuckoo had been singing five days; the lanes and fields, the woods and the village green were as Joseph's coat, so varied and so bright the foliage, from golden oak-buds to the brilliant little lime-tree leaves, the feathery green shoots of larches, and the already darkening bunches of the sycamores. The earth was dry—no rain for a fortnight—when the cars containing the brown-clad men and a recruiting band drew up before the Inn. Here were clustered the farmers, the innkeeper, the grey-haired postman; by the Church gate and before the schoolyard were knots of girls and children, schoolmistress, schoolmaster, parson; and down on the lower green a group of likely youths, an old labourer or two, and apart from human beings as was his wont, the little cowman in brown corduroys tied below the knee, and an old waistcoat, the sleeves of his blue shirt dotted with pink, rolled up to the elbows of his brown arms. So he stood, his brown neck and shaven-looking head quite bare, with his bit of stick wedged between his waist and the ground, staring with all his light-lashed water-blue eyes from under the thatch of his forelock.

The speeches rolled forth glib; the khaki-clad men drank their second fill that morning of coffee and cider; the little cowman stood straight and still, his head drawn back. Two figures—officers, men who had been at the front—detached themselves and came towards the group of likely youths. These wavered a little, were silent, sniggered, stood their ground—the khaki-clad figures passed among them. Hackneyed words, jests, the touch of flattery, changing swiftly to chaff—all the customary performance, hollow and pathetic; and then the two figures re-emerged, their hands clenched, their eyes shifting here and there, their lips drawn back in fixed smiles. They had failed, and were trying to hide it. They must not show contempt—the young slackers might yet come in, when the band played.

The cars were filled again, the band struck up: 'It's a long long way to Tipperary.'

And at the edge of the green within two yards of the car's dusty passage the little cowman stood apart and stared. His face was red. Behind him they were cheering—the parson and farmers, school children, girls, even the group of youths. He alone did not cheer, but his face grew still more red. When the dust above the road and the distant blare of Tipperary had dispersed and died, he walked back to the farm dotting from one to other of his short feet. All that afternoon and evening he spoke no word; but the flush seemed to have settled in his face for good and all. He milked some cows, but forgot to bring the pails up. Two of his precious cows he left unmilked till their distressful lowing caused the farmer's wife to go down and see. There he was standing against a gate moving his brown neck from side to side like an animal in pain, oblivious seemingly of everything. She spoke to him:

"What's matter, Tom?" All he could answer was:

"I'se goin', I'se goin'." She milked the cows herself.

For the next three days he could settle to nothing, leaving his jobs half done, speaking to no one save to say:

"I'se goin'; I'se got to go." Even the beasts looked at him surprised.

On the Saturday the farmer having consulted with his wife, said quietly:

"Well, Tom, ef yu want to go, yu shall. I'll drive 'ee down Monday. Us won't du nothin' to keep yu back."

The little cowman nodded. But he was restless as ever all through that Sunday, eating nothing.

On Monday morning arrayed in his best clothes he got into the dog-cart. There, without good-bye to anyone, not even to his beasts, he sat staring straight before him, square, and jolting up and down beside the farmer, who turned on him now and then a dubious almost anxious eye.

So they drove the eleven miles to the recruiting station. He got down, entered, the farmer with him.

"Well, my lad," they asked him, "what d'you want to join?"

"Royal Marines."

It was a shock, coming from the short, square figure of such an obvious landsman. The farmer took him by the arm.

"Why, yu'm a Devon man, Tom, better take county regiment. An't they gude enough for yu?"

Shaking his head he answered: "Royal Marines."

Was it the glamour of the words or the Royal Marine he had once seen, that moved him to wish to join that outlandish corps? Who shall say? There was the wish, immovable; they took him to the recruiting station for the Royal Marines.

Stretching up his short, square body, and blowing out his cheeks to increase his height, he was put before the reading board. His eyes were splendid; little that passed in hedgerows or the heaven, in woods or on the hillsides, could escape them. They asked him to read the print.

Staring, he answered: "L."

"No, my lad, you're guessing."

"L."

The farmer plucked at the recruiting officer's sleeve, his face was twitching, and he whispered hoarsely:

"'E don' know 'is alphabet."

The officer turned and contemplated that short square figure with the browned face so reminiscent of a withered baby, and the little blue eyes staring out under the dusty forelock. Then he grunted, and going up to him, laid a hand on his shoulder.

"Your heart's all right, my lad, but you can't pass."

The little cowman looked at him, turned, and went straight out. An hour later he sat again beside the farmer on the way home, staring before him and jolting up and down.

"They won't get me," he said suddenly: "I can fight, but I'se not goin'." A fire of resentment seemed to have been lit within him. That evening he ate his tea, and next day settled down again among his beasts. But whenever, now, the war was mentioned, he would look up with his puckered smile which seemed to have in it a resentful amusement, and say:

"They a'nt got me yet."

His dumb sacrifice passing their comprehension, had been rejected—or so it seemed to him He could not understand that they had spared him. Why! He was as good as they! His pride was hurt. No! They should not get him now!

CHAPTER VIII

THE PEACE MEETING

Colin Wilderton, coming from the West on his way to the Peace Meeting, fell in with John Rudstock, coming from the North, and they walked on together. After they had commented on the news from Russia and the inflation of money, Rudstock said abruptly:

"We shall have a queer meeting, I expect."

"God knows!" answered Wilderton.

And both smiled, conscious that they were uneasy, but predetermined not to show it under any circumstances. Their smiles were different, for Rudstock was a black-browed man, with dark beard and strong, thick figure, and Wilderton a very light-built, grey-haired man, with kindly eyes and no health. He had supported the war an immense time, and had only recently changed his attitude. In common with all men of warm feelings, he had at first been profoundly moved by the violation of Belgium. The horrors of the German advance through that little country and through France, to which he was temperamentally attached, had stirred in him a vigorous detestation, freely expressed in many ways. Extermination, he had felt all those early months, was hardly good enough for brutes who could commit such crimes against humanity and justice; and his sense of the need for signal defeat of a noxious force riding rough-shod over the hard-won decency of human life had survived well into the third year of the war. He hardly knew, himself, when his feeling had begun—not precisely to change, but to run, as it were, in a different channel. A man of generous instincts, artistic tastes, and unsteady nerves too thinly coated with that God-given assurance which alone fits a man for knowing what is good for the world, he had become gradually haunted by the thought that he was not laying down his own life, but only the lives of his own and other peoples' sons. And the consideration that he was laying them down for the benefit of their own future had lost its grip on him. At moments he was still able to see that the war he had so long supported had not yet attained sufficient defeat of the Prussian military machine to guarantee that future; but his pity and distress for all these young lives, cut down without a chance to flower, had grown till he had become, as it were, a gambler. What good—he would think—to secure the future of the young in a Europe which would soon have no young! Every country was suffering hideously—the criminal country not least, thank God! Suppose the war were to go on for another year, two, three years, and then stop from sheer exhaustion of both sides, while all the time these boys were being killed and maimed, for nothing more, perhaps, than could be obtained to-day. What then? True, the Government promised victory, but they never promised it within a year. Governments did not die; what if they were to go on promising it a year hence, till everybody else was dead! Did history ever show that victory in the present could guarantee the future? And even if not so openly defeated as was desirable, this damnable Prussianism had got such a knock that it could never again do what it had in the past. These last, however, were but side reflections, toning down for him the fact that his nerves could no longer stand this vicarious butchery of youth. And so he had gradually become that "traitor to his country, a weak-kneed Peace by Negotiation man." Physically his knees really were weak, and he used to smile a wry smile when he read the expression.

John Rudstock, of vigorous physique, had opposed the war, on principle, from the start, not because, any more than Wilderton, he approved of Prussianism, but because, as an essentially combative personality, he opposed everything that was supported by a majority; the greater the majority, the more bitterly he opposed it; and no one would have been more astonished than he at hearing that this was his principle. He preferred to put it that he did not believe in opposing Force by Force. In peace-time he was a "stalwart," in war-time a "renegade."

The street leading to the chapel which had been engaged seemed quiet enough. Designed to make an impression on public opinion, every care had been taken that the meeting should not attract the public eye. God's protection had been enlisted, but two policemen also stood at the entrance, and half a dozen others were suspiciously near by. A thin trickle of persons, mostly women, were passing through the door. Colin Wilderton, making his way up the aisle to the platform, wrinkled his nose, thinking: "Stuffy in here." It had always been his misfortune to love his neighbours individually, but to dislike them in a bunch. On the platform some fifteen men and women were already gathered. He seated himself modestly in the back row, while John Rudstock, less retiring, took his place at the chairman's right hand.

The speakers began with a precipitancy hardly usual at a public meeting. Wilderton listened, and thought: "Dreadfully cliché; why can't someone say straight out that boys enough have been killed?" He had become conscious of a muttering noise, too, as of the tide coming in on a heavy wind; it broke suddenly into component parts—human voices clamouring outside. He heard blows raining on the door, saw sticks smashing in the windows. The audience had risen to its feet, some rushing to defend the doors, others standing irresolute. John Rudstock was holding up the chair he had been sitting on. Wilderton had just time to think: "I thought so," when a knot of young men in khaki burst into the chapel, followed by a crowd. He knew he was not much good in a scrimmage, but he placed himself at once in front of the nearest woman. At that moment, however, some soldiers, pouring through a side-door, invaded the platform from behind, and threw him down the steps. He arrived at the bottom with a bump, and was unable to get up because of the crowd around him. Someone fell over him; it was Rudstock, swearing horribly. He still had the chair in his hand, for it hit Wilderton a nasty blow. The latter saw his friend recover his feet and swing the weapon, and with each swing down went some friend or foe, until he had cleared quite a space round him. Wilderton, still weak and dizzy from his fall, sat watching this Homeric battle. Chairs, books, stools, sticks were flying at Rudstock, who parried them, or diverted their course so that they carried on and hit Wilderton, or crashed against the platform. He heard Rudstock roar like a lion, and saw him advance, swinging his chair; down went two young men in khaki, down went a third in mufti; a very tall young soldier, also armed with a chair, dashed forward, and the two fought in single combat. Wilderton had got on his feet by now, and, adjusting his eyeglass, for he could see little without, he caught up a hymn-book, and, flinging it at the crowd with all his force, shouted: "Hoo-bloodyray!" and followed with his fists clenched. One of them encountered what must have been the jaw of an Australian, it was so hard against his hand; he received a vicious punch in the ribs and was again seated on the ground. He could still hear his friend roaring, and the crash of chairs meeting in mid-air. Something fell heavily on him. It was Rudstock—he was insensible. There was a momentary lull, and peering up as best he could from underneath the body, Wilderton saw that the platform had been cleared of all its original inhabitants, and was occupied mainly by youths in navy-blue and khaki. A voice called out:

"Order! Silence!"

Rubbing Rudstock's temples with brandy from a flask which he had had the foresight to slip into his pocket, he listened as best he could, with the feet of the crowd jostling his anatomy.

"Here we are, boys," the voice was saying, "and here we'll always be when these treacherous blighters try their games on. No peace, no peace at any price! We've got to show them that we won't have it. Leave the women alone—though they ought to be ashamed of themselves; but for the men—the skunks—shooting's too good for them. Let them keep off the course or we'll make them. We've broken up this meeting, and we'll break up every meeting that tries to talk of peace. Three cheers for the old flag!"

During the cheers which followed Wilderton was discovering signs of returning consciousness in his friend. Rudstock had begun to breathe heavily, and, pouring some brandy into his mouth, he propped him up as best he could against a wooden structure, which he suddenly perceived to be the chapel's modest pulpit. A thought came to his dazed brain. If he could get up into that, as if he had dropped from Heaven, they might almost listen to him. He disengaged his legs from under Rudstock, and began crawling up the steps on hands and knees. Once in the pulpit he sat on the floor below the level of visibility, getting his breath, and listening to the cheers. Then, smoothing his hair, he rose, and waited for the cheers to stop. He had calculated rightly. His sudden appearance, his grey hair, eyeglass, and smile deceived them for a moment. There was a hush.

"Boys!" he said, "listen to me a second, I want to ask you something. What on earth do you think we came here for? Simply and solely because we can't bear to go on seeing you killed day after day, month after month, year after year. That's all, and it's Christ's truth. Amen!"

A strange gasp and mutter greeted this little speech; then a dull voice called out:

"Pro-German!"

Wilderton flung up his hand.

"The Germans to hell!" he said simply.

The dull voice repeated:

"Pro-German!" And the speaker on the platform called out: "Come out of that! When we want you to beg us off we'll let you know."

Wilderton spun round to him.

"You're all wonderful!" he began, but a hymn-book hit him fearfully on the forehead, and he sank down into the bottom of the pulpit. This last blow, coming on the top of so many others, had deprived him of intelligent consciousness; he was but vaguely aware of more speeches, cheers, and tramplings, then of a long hush, and presently found himself walking out of the chapel door between Rudstock and a policeman. It was not the door by which they had entered, and led to an empty courtyard.

"Can you walk?" said the policeman.

Wilderton nodded.

"Then walk off!" said the policeman, and withdrew again into the house of God.

They walked, holding each other's arms, a little unsteadily at first. Rudstock had a black eye and a cut on his ear, the blood from which had stained his collar and matted his beard. Wilderton's coat was torn, his forehead bruised, his cheek swollen, and he had a pain in his back which prevented him from walking very upright. They did not speak, but in an archway did what they could with pins and handkerchiefs, and by turning up Rudstock's coat collar, to regain something of respectability. When they were once more under way Rudstock said coldly:

"I heard you. You should have spoken for yourself. I came, as you know, because I don't believe in opposing force by force. At the next peace meeting we hold I shall make that plainer."

Wilderton murmured:

"Yes, yes; I saw you—I'm sure you will. I apologise; I was carried away."

Rudstock went on in a deep voice:

"As for those young devils, they may die to a man if they like! Take my advice and let them alone."

Wilderton smiled on the side which was not swollen.

"Yes," he said sadly, "it does seem difficult to persuade them to go on living. Ah, well!"

"Ah, well!" he said again, five minutes later, "they're wonderful—poor young beggars! I'm very unhappy, Rudstock!"

"I'm not," said Rudstock, "I've enjoyed it in a way! Good-night!"

They shook hands, screwing up their mouths with pain, for their fists were badly bruised, and parted, Rudstock going to the North, Wilderton to the West.

CHAPTER IX

"THE DOG IT WAS THAT DIED"

Until the great war was over I had no idea that some of us who stayed at home made the great sacrifice.

My friend Harburn is, or rather was, a Northumbrian, or some kind of Northerner, a stocky man of perhaps fifty, with close-clipped grizzled hair and moustache, and a deep-coloured face. He was a neighbour of mine in the country, and we had the same kind of dogs—Airedales, never less than three at a time, so that for breeding purposes we were useful to each other. We often, too, went up to Town by the same train. His occupation was one which gave him opportunity of prominence in public life, but until the war he took little advantage of this, sunk in a kind of bluff indifferentism which was almost cynical. I used to look on him as a typically good-natured blunt Englishman, rather enjoying his cynicism, and appreciating his open-air tendencies—for he was a devotee of golf, and fond of shooting when he had the chance; a good companion, too, with an open hand to people in distress. He was unmarried, and dwelled in a bungalow-like house not far from mine, and next door to a German family called Holsteig, who had lived in England nearly twenty years. I knew them pretty well also—a very united trio, father, mother, and one son. The father, who came from Hanover, was something in the City, the mother was Scotch, and the son—the one I knew best and liked most—had just left his public school. This youth had a frank, open, blue-eyed face, and thick light hair brushed back without a parting—a very attractive, slightly Norwegian-looking type. His mother was devoted to him; she was a real West Highlander, slight, with dark hair going grey, high cheekbones, a sweet but rather ironical smile, and those grey eyes which have second sight in them. I several times met Harburn at their house, for he would go in to play billiards with Holsteig in the evenings, and the whole family were on very friendly terms with him.

The third morning after we had declared war on Germany Harburn, Holsteig, and I went up to Town in the same carriage. Harburn and I talked freely. But Holsteig, a fair, well-set-up man of about fifty, with a pointed beard and blue eyes like his son, sat immersed in his paper till Harburn said suddenly:

"I say, Holsteig, is it true that your boy was going off to join the German army?"

Holsteig looked up.

"Yes," he said. "He was born in Germany; he's liable to military service. But thank heaven, it isn't possible for him to go."

"But his mother?" said Harburn. "She surely wouldn't have let him?"

"She was very miserable, of course, but she thought duty came first."

"Duty! Good God!—my dear man! Half British, and living in this country all his life! I never heard of such a thing!" Holsteig shrugged his shoulders.

"In a crisis like this, what can you do except follow the law strictly? He is of military age and a German subject. We were thinking of his honour; but of course we're most thankful he can't get over to Germany."

"Well, I'm damned!" said Harburn. "You Germans are too bally conscientious altogether."

Holsteig did not answer.

I travelled back with Harburn the same evening, and he said to me:

"Once a German, always a German. Didn't that chap Holsteig astonish you this morning? In spite of living here so long and marrying a British wife, his sympathies are dead German, you see."

"Well," I replied; "put yourself in his place."

"I can't; I could never have lived in Germany. I wonder," he added reflectively, "I wonder if the chap's all right, Cumbermere?"

"Of course he's all right." Which was the wrong thing to say to Harburn if one wanted to re-establish his confidence in the Holsteigs, as I certainly did, for I liked them and was sure of their good faith. If I had said: "Of course he's a spy"—I should have rallied all Harburn's confidence in Holsteig, for he was naturally contradictious.

I only mention this little passage to show how early Harburn's thoughts began to turn to the subject which afterwards completely absorbed and inspired him till he died for his country.

I am not sure what paper first took up the question of interning all the Huns; but I fancy the point was raised originally rather from the instinct, deeply implanted in so many journals, for what would please the public, than out of any deep animus. At all events I remember meeting a sub-editor, who told me he had been opening letters of approval all the morning. "Never," said he, "have we had a stunt catch on so quickly. 'Why should that bally German round the corner get my custom?' and so forth. Britain for the British!"

"Rather bad luck," I said, "on people who've paid us the compliment of finding this the best country to live in!"

"Bad luck, no doubt," he replied, "mais la guerre c'est la guerre. You know Harburn, don't you? Did you see the article he wrote? By Jove, he pitched it strong."

When next I met Harburn himself, he began talking on this subject at once.

"Mark my words, Cumbermere, I'll have every German out of this country." His grey eyes seemed to glint with the snap and spark as of steel and flint and tinder; and I felt I was in the presence of a man who had brooded so over the German atrocities in Belgium that he was possessed by a sort of abstract hate.

"Of course," I said, "there have been many spies, but—"

"Spies and ruffians," he cried, "the whole lot of them."

"How many Germans do you know personally?" I asked him.

"Thank God! Not a dozen."

"And are they spies and ruffians?"

He looked at me and laughed, but that laugh was uncommonly like a snarl.

"You go in for 'fairness,'" he said; "and all that slop; take 'em by the throat—it's the only way."

It trembled on the tip of my tongue to ask him whether he meant to take the Holsteigs by the throat, but I swallowed it, for fear of doing them an injury. I was feeling much the same general abhorrence myself, and had to hold myself in all the time for fear it should gallop over my commonsense. But Harburn, I could see, was giving it full rein. His whole manner and personality somehow had changed. He had lost geniality, and that good-humoured cynicism which had made him an attractive companion; he was as if gnawed at inwardly—in a word, he already had a fixed idea.

Now, a cartoonist like myself has got to be interested in the psychology of men and things, and I brooded over Harburn, for it seemed to me remarkable that one whom I had always associated with good humour and bluff indifference should be thus obsessed. And I formed this theory about him: 'Here'—I said to myself—'is one of Cromwell's Ironsides, born out of his age. In the slack times of peace he discovered no outlet for the grim within him—his fire could never be lighted by love, therefore he drifted in the waters of indifferentism. Now suddenly in this grizzly time he has found himself, a new man, girt and armed by this new passion of hate; stung and uplifted, as it were, by the sight of that which he can smite with a whole heart. It's deeply interesting'—I said to myself—'Who could have dreamed of such a reincarnation; for what on the surface could possibly be less alike than an 'Ironside,' and Harburn as I've known him up to now?' And I used his face for the basis of a cartoon which represented a human weather-vane continually pointing to the East, no matter from what quarter the wind blew. He recognised himself, and laughed when he saw me—rather pleased, in fact, but in that laugh there was a sort of truculence, as if the man had the salt taste of blood at the back of his mouth.

"Ah!" he said, "you may joke about it, but I've got my teeth into them all right. The swine!"

And there was no doubt he had—the man had become a force; unhappy Germans, a few of them spies, no doubt, but the great majority as certainly innocent, were being wrenched from their trades and families, and piled into internment camps all day and every day. And the faster they were piled in, the higher grew his stock, as a servant of his country. I'm sure he did not do it to gain credit; the thing was a crusade to him, something sacred—'his bit'; but I believe he also felt for the first time in his life that he was really living, getting out of life the full of its juice. Was he not smiting hip and thigh? He longed, I am sure, to be in the thick of the actual fighting, but age debarred him, and he was not of that more sensitive type which shrinks from smiting the defenceless if it cannot smite anything stronger. I remember saying to him once:

"Harburn, do you ever think of the women and children of your victims?"

He drew his lips back, and I saw how excellent his teeth were.

"The women are worse than the men, I believe," he said. "I'd put them in, too, if I could. As for the children, they're all the better for being without fathers of that kidney."

He really was a little mad on the subject; no more so, of course, than any other man with a fixed idea, but certainly no less.

In those days I was here, there, and everywhere, and had let my country cottage, so I saw nothing of the Holsteigs, and indeed had pretty well forgotten their existence. But coming back at the end of 1917 from a long spell with the Red Cross I found among my letters one from Mrs. Holsteig:

"Dear Mr. Cumbermere,

You were always so friendly to us that I have summoned up courage to write this letter. You know perhaps that my husband was interned over a year ago, and repatriated last September; he has lost everything, of course; but so far he is well and able to get along in Germany. Harold and I have been jogging on here as best we can on my own little income—'Huns in our midst' as we are, we see practically nobody. What a pity we cannot all look into each other's hearts, isn't it? I used to think we were a 'fair-play' people, but I have learned the bitter truth—that there is no such thing when pressure comes. It's much worse for Harold than for me; he feels his paralysed position intensely, and would, I'm sure, really rather be 'doing his bit' as an interned, than be at large, subject to everyone's suspicion and scorn. But I am terrified all the time that they will intern him. You used to be intimate with Mr. Harburn. We have not seen him since the first autumn of the war, but we know that he has been very active in the agitation, and is very powerful in this matter. I have wondered whether he can possibly realise what this indiscriminate internment of the innocent means to the families of the interned. Could you not find a chance to try and make him understand? If he and a few others were to stop hounding on the government, it would cease, for the authorities must know perfectly well that all the dangerous have been disposed of long ago. You have no notion how lonely one feels in one's native land nowadays; if I should lose Harold too I think I might go under, though that has never been my habit.

Believe me, dear Mr. Cumbermere,
Most truly yours
HELEN HOLSTEIG."

On receiving this letter I was moved by compassion, for it required no stretch of imagination to picture the life of that lonely British mother and her son; and I thought very carefully over the advisability of speaking to Harburn, and consulted the proverbs: "Speech is silver, but Silence is golden—When in doubt play trumps." "Second thoughts are best—He who hesitates is lost." "Look before you leap—Delays are dangerous." They balanced so perfectly that I had recourse to Commonsense, which told me to abstain. But meeting Harburn at the Club a few days later and finding him in a genial mood, I let impulse prevail, and said:

"By the way, Harburn, you remember the Holsteigs? I had a letter from poor Mrs. Holsteig the other day; she seems terrified that they'll intern her son, that particularly nice boy. Don't you think it's time you let up on these unhappy people?"

The moment I reached the word Holsteig I saw I had made a mistake, and only went on because to have stopped at that would have been worse still. The hair had bristled up on his back, as it were, and he said:

"Holsteig? That young pup who was off to join the German army if he could? By George, is he at large still? This Government will never learn. I'll remember him."

"Harburn," I stammered, "I spoke of this in confidence. The boy is half British, and a friend of mine. I thought he was a friend of yours too."

"Of mine?" he said. "No thank you. No mongrels for me. As to confidence, Cumbermere, there's no such thing in war time over what concerns the country's safety."

"Good God!" I exclaimed. "You really are crazy on this subject. That boy—with his bringing-up!"

He grinned. "We're taking no risks," he said, "and making no exceptions. The British army or an internment camp. I'll see that he gets the alternatives."

"If you do," I said, rising, "we cease to be friends. I won't have my confidence abused."

"Oh! Hang it all!" he grumbled; "sit down! We must all do our duty."

"You once complained to Holsteig himself of that German peculiarity."

He laughed. "I did," he said; "I remember—in the train. I've changed since then. That pup ought to be in with all the other swine-hounds. But let it go."

There the matter rested, for he had said: "Let it go," and he was a man of his word. It was, however, a lesson to me not to meddle with men of temperament so different from my own. I wrote to young Holsteig and asked him to come and lunch with me. He thanked me, but could not, of course, being confined to a five-mile radius. Really anxious to see him, I motorbiked down to their house. I found a very changed youth; moody and introspective, thoroughly forced in upon himself, and growing bitter. He had been destined for his father's business, and, marooned as he was by his nationality, had nothing to do but raise vegetables in their garden and read poetry and philosophy—not occupations to take a young man out of himself. Mrs. Holsteig, whose nerves were evidently at cracking point, had become extremely bitter, and lost all power of seeing the war as a whole. All the ugly human qualities and hard people which the drive and pressure of a great struggle inevitably bring to the top seemed viewed by her now as if they were the normal character of her fellow countrymen, and she made no allowance for the fact that those fellow countrymen had not commenced this struggle, nor for the certainty that the same ugly qualities and hard people were just as surely to the fore in every other of the fighting countries. The certainty she felt about her husband's honour had made her regard his internment and subsequent repatriation as a personal affront, as well as a wicked injustice. Her tall thin figure and high-cheekboned face seemed to have been scorched and withered by some inner flame; she could not have been a wholesome companion for her boy in that house, empty even of servants. I spent a difficult afternoon in muzzling my sense of proportion, and journeyed back to Town sore, but very sorry.

I was off again with the Red Cross shortly after, and did not return to England till August of 1918. I was unwell, and went down to my cottage, now free to me again. The influenza epidemic was raging, and there I developed a mild attack; when I was convalescent my first visitor was Harburn, who had come down to his bungalow for a summer holiday. He had not been in the room five minutes before he was off on his favourite topic. My nerves must have been on edge from illness, for I cannot express the disgust with which I listened to him on that occasion. He seemed to me just like a dog who mumbles and chews a mouldy old bone with a sort of fury. There was a kind of triumph about him, too, which was unpleasant, though not surprising, for he was more of a 'force' than ever. 'God save me from the fixed idea!' I thought, when he was gone. That evening I asked my old housekeeper if she had seen young Mr. Holsteig lately.

"Oh! no," she said; "he's been put away this five month. Mrs. 'Olsteig goes up once a week to see 'im, 'Olsteig. She's nigh out of her mind, poor lady—the baker says; that fierce she is about the Gover'ment."

I confess I could not bring myself to go and see her.

About a month after the armistice had been signed I came down to my cottage again. Harburn was in the same train, and he gave me a lift from the station. He was more like his old good-humoured self, and asked me to dinner the next day. It was the first time I had met him since the victory. We had a most excellent repast, and drank the health of the Future in some of his oldest port. Only when we had drawn up to the blazing wood fire in that softly lighted room, with our glasses beside us and two Airedales asleep at our feet, did he come round to his hobby.

"What do you think?" he said, suddenly leaning towards the flames, "some of these blazing sentimentalists want to release our Huns. But I've put my foot on it; they won't get free till they're out of this country and back in their precious Germany." And I saw the familiar spark and smoulder in his eyes.

"Harburn," I said, moved by an impulse which I couldn't resist, "I think you ought to take a pill."

He stared at me.

"This way madness lies," I went on. "Hate is a damned insidious disease; men's souls can't stand very much of it without going pop. You want purging."

He laughed.

"Hate! I thrive on it. The more I hate the brutes, the better I feel. Here's to the death of every cursed Hun!"

I looked at him steadily. "I often think," I said, "that there could have been no more unhappy men on earth than Cromwell's Ironsides, or the red revolutionaries in France, when their work was over and done with."

"What's that to do with me?" he said, amazed.

"They too smote out of sheer hate, and came to an end of their smiting. When a man's occupation's gone—"

"You're drivelling!" he said sharply.

"Far from it," I answered, nettled. "Yours is a curious case, Harburn. Most of our professional Hun-haters have found it a good stunt, or are merely weak sentimentalists; they can drop it easily enough when it ceases to be a good stunt, or a parrot's war-cry. You can't; with you it's mania, religion. When the tide ebbs and leaves you high and dry—"

He struck his fist on the arm of his chair, upsetting his glass and awakening the Airedale at his feet.

"I won't let it ebb," he said; "I'm going on with this—Mark me!"

"Remember Canute!" I muttered. "May I have some more port?" I had got up to fill my glass when I saw to my astonishment that a woman was standing in the long window which opened on to the verandah. She had evidently only just come in, for she was still holding the curtain in her hand. It was Mrs. Holsteig, with her fine grey hair blown about her face, looking strange and almost ghostly in a grey gown. Harburn had not seen her, so I went quickly towards her, hoping to get her to go out again as silently, and speak to me on the verandah; but she held up her hand with a gesture as if she would push me back, and said:

"Forgive my interrupting; I came to speak to that man."

Startled by the sound of her voice, Harburn jumped up and spun round towards it.

"Yes," she repeated quite quietly; "I came to speak to you; I came to put my curse on you. Many have put their curses on you silently; I do so to your face. My son lies between life and death in your prison— your prison. Whether he lives or dies I curse you for what you have done to poor wives and mothers—to British wives and mothers. Be for ever accursed! Good-night!"

She let the curtain fall, and had vanished before Harburn had time to reach the window. She vanished so swiftly and silently, she had spoken so quietly, that both he and I stood rubbing our eyes and ears.

"A bit theatrical!" he said at last.

"Perhaps," I answered slowly; "but you have been cursed by a live Scotswoman. Look at those dogs!"

The two Airedales were standing stock-still with the hair bristling on their backs.

Harburn suddenly laughed, and it jarred the whole room.

"By George!" he said, "I believe that's actionable."

But I was not in that mood, and said tartly:

"If it is, we are all food for judges."

He laughed again, this time uneasily, slammed the window to, bolted it, and sat down again in his chair.

"He's got the 'flue,' I suppose," he said. "She must think me a prize sort of idiot to have come here with such tomfoolery."

But our evening was spoiled, and I took my leave almost at once. I went out into the roupy raw December night pondering deeply. Harburn had made light of it, and though I suppose no man likes being cursed to his face in the presence of a friend, I felt his skin was quite thick enough to stand it. Besides, it was too cheap and crude a way of carrying on. Anybody can go into his neighbour's house and curse him—and no bones broken. And yet—what she had said was no doubt true; hundreds of women—of his fellow countrywomen—must silently have put their curse on one who had been the chief compeller of their misery. Still, he had put his curse on the Huns and their belongings, and I felt he was man enough to take what he had given. 'No,' I thought, 'she has only fanned the flame of his hate. But, by Jove! that's just it! Her curse has fortified my prophecy!' It was of his own state of mind that he would perish; and she had whipped and deepened that state of mind. And, odd as it may seem, I felt quite sorry for him, as one is for a poor dog that goes mad, does what harm he can, and dies. I lay awake that night a long time thinking of him, and of that unhappy, half-crazed mother, whose son lay between life and death.

Next day I went to see her, but she was up in London, hovering round the cage of her son, no doubt. I heard from her, however, some days later, thanking me for coming, and saying he was out of danger. But she made no allusion to that evening visit. Perhaps she was ashamed of it. Perhaps she was demented when she came, and had no remembrance thereof.

Soon after this I went to Belgium to illustrate a book on Reconstruction, and found such subjects that I was not back in Town till the late summer of 1919. Going into my Club one day I came on Harburn in the smoking-room. The curse had not done him much harm, it seemed, for he looked the picture of health.

"Well, how are you?" I said. "You look at the top of your form."

"Never better," he replied.

"Do you remember our last evening together?"

He uttered a sort of gusty grunt, and did not answer.

"That boy recovered," I said. "What's happened to him and his mother, since?"

"The ironical young brute! I've just had this from him." And he handed me a letter with the Hanover post mark.

"Dear Mr. Harburn,

It was only on meeting my mother here yesterday that I learned of her visit to you one evening last December. I wish to apologise for it, since it was my illness which caused her to so forget herself. I owe you a deep debt of gratitude for having been at least part means of giving me the most wonderful experience of my life. In that camp of sorrow—where there was sickness of mind and body such as I am sure you have never seen or realised, such endless hopeless mental anguish of poor huddled creatures turning and turning on themselves year after year—I learned to forget myself, and to do my little best for them. And I learned, and I hope I shall never forget it, that feeling for one's fellow creatures is all that stands between man and death; I was going fast the other way before I was sent there. I thank you from my heart, and beg to remain,

Very faithfully yours
HAROLD HOLSTEIG."

I put it down, and said:

"That's not ironical. He means it."

"Bosh!" said Harburn, with the old spark and smoulder in his eyes. "He's pulling my leg—the swinelet Hun!"

"He is not, Harburn; I assure you."

Harburn got up. "He is; I tell you he is. Ah! Those brutes! Well! I haven't done with them yet."

And I heard the snap of his jaw, and saw his eyes fixed fiercely on some imaginary object. I changed the subject hurriedly, and soon took my departure. But going down the steps, an old jingle came into my head, and has hardly left it since:

"The man recovered from the bite, The dog it was that died."

CHAPTER X

IN HEAVEN AND EARTH

We were yarning after dinner, and, whether because three of us were fishermen, or simply that we were all English, our yarns were taking a competitive turn. The queerest thing seen during the War was the subject of our tongues, and it was not till after several tit-bits had been digested that Mallinson, the painter, ill and ironical, blue-eyed, and with a fair pointed beard, took his pipe out of his mouth, and said:

"Well, you chaps, what I saw last week down in Kent takes some beating. I'd been sketching in a hay-field, and was just making back along the top hedge to the lane when I heard a sound from the other side like a man's crying. I put my eye to a gap, and there, about three yards in, was a grey-haired bloke in a Norfolk jacket and flannel trousers, digging like a fiend, and crying like a baby—blowing, and gasping and sobbing, tears and sweat rolling down into his beard like rivers. He'd plunge his pick in, scratch, and shovel, and hack at the roots as if for dear life—he was making the hole too close to the hedge, of course—and all the time carrying on like that. I thought he must be digging his own grave at least. Suddenly he put his pick down, and there just under the hedge I saw a dead brown dog, lying on its side, all limp. I never see a dead animal myself, you know, without a bit of a choke; they're so soft, and lissom; the peace, and the pity—a sort of look of: "Why—why—when I was so alive?" Well, this elderly Johnny took a good squint at it, to see if the hole was big enough, then off he went again, sobbing and digging like a fiend. It was really a bit too weird, and I mouched off. But when I'd gone about half a mile, I got an attack of the want-to-knows, came back, and sneaked along the hedge. There he was still, but he had finished, and was having a mop round, and putting the last touches to a heap of stones. I strolled up, and said:

'Hot work, Sir, digging, this weather!'

He was a good-looking old grey-beard, with an intellectual face, high forehead and all that.

'I'm not used to it,' he said, looking at his blisters.

'Been burying a dog? Horrid job that!—favourite, I'm afraid.'

He seemed in two minds whether to shut me up and move off, but he didn't.

'Yes,' he said; 'it's cut me up horribly. I never condemned a creature to death before. And dogs seem to know.'

'Ah! They're pretty uncanny,' I said, for I wasn't going to let on, of course, that I had seen him.

'I wouldn't have done it but for the War,' he muttered; 'but she stole eggs, poor thing; you couldn't break her of it. She ate three times as much as any other dog, too, and in spite of it was always a perfect skeleton—something wrong inside. The sort of dog, you know, no one would take, or treat decently if they did. Bad habits of every kind, poor dear. I bought her because she was being starved. But she trusted me, that's why I feel so like a murderer. When the Vet and I were in the yard discussing her, she knew there was something wrong—she kept looking at my face. I very nearly went back on it; only, having got him out on purpose, I was ashamed to. We brought her down here, and on the way she found the remains of a rabbit about a week old—that was one of her accomplishments—bringing me the most fearful offal. She brought it up wagging her tail—as much as to say: 'See—I am some use!' The Vet tied her up here and took his gun; she wagged her tail at that, too; and I ran away. When the shot came, my own little spaniel fawned on me—they are uncanny—licked me all over, never was so gushing, seemed saying: 'What awful power you have! I do love you! You wouldn't do that to me, would you? We've got rid of that other one, though!' When I came back here to bury the poor thing, and saw her lying on her side so still, I made a real fool of myself. I was patting her an hour ago, talking to her as if she were a human being. Judas!'"

Mallinson put his pipe back into his mouth. "Just think of it!" he said: "The same creatures who are blowing each other to little bits all the time, bombing babies, roasting fellow creatures in the air and cheering while they roast, working day and night to inflict every imaginable kind of horror on other men exactly like themselves—these same chaps are capable of feeling like that about shooting a wretched ill cur of a dog, no good to anybody. There are more things in Heaven and Earth—!" And he relit his pipe, which had gone out.

His yarn took the prize.

CHAPTER XI

THE MOTHER STONE

It was after dinner, and five elderly Englishmen were discussing the causes of the war.

"Well," said Travers, a big, fresh-coloured grey-beard, with little twinkling eyes and very slow speech, "you gentlemen know more about it than I do, but I bet you I can lay my finger on the cause of the war at any minute."

There was an instant clamour of jeering. But a man called Askew, who knew Travers well, laughed and said: "Come, let's have it!" Travers turned those twinkling little eyes of his slowly round the circle, and with heavy, hesitating modesty began:

"Well, Mr. Askew, it was in '67 or '68 that this happened to a great big feller of my acquaintance named Ray—one of those fellers, you know, that are always on the look-out to make their fortunes and never do. This Ray was coming back south one day after a huntin' trip he'd been in what's now called Bechuanaland, and he was in a pretty bad way when he walked one evenin' into the camp of one of those wanderin' Boers. That class of Boer has disappeared now. They had no farms of their own, but just moved on with their stock and their boys; and when they came to good pasture they'd outspan and stay there till they'd cleared it out—and then trek on again. Well, this old Boer told Ray to come right in, and take a meal; and heaven knows what it was made of, for those old Boers, they'd eat the devil himself without onion sauce, and relish him. After the meal the old Boer and Ray sat smokin' and yarnin' in the door of the tent, because in those days these wanderin' Boers used tents. Right close by in the front, the children were playin' in the dust, a game like marbles, with three or four round stones, and they'd pitch 'em up to another stone they called the Moer-Klip, or Mother-stone—one, two, and pick up—two, three, and pick up—you know the game of marbles. Well, the sun was settin' and presently Ray noticed this Moer-Klip that they were pitchin' 'em up to, shinin'; and he looked at it, and he said to the old Boer: 'What's that stone the children are playin' with?' And the old Boer looked at him and looked at the stone, and said: 'It's just a stone,' and went on smokin'.

"Well, Ray went down on his knees and picked up the stone, and weighed it in his hand. About the size of a hazel-nut it was, and looked—well, it looked like a piece of alum; but the more he looked at it, the more he thought: 'By Jove, I believe it's a diamond!'

"So he said to the old Boer: 'Where did the children get this stone?' And the old Boer said: 'Oh! the shepherd picked it up somewhere.' And Ray said: 'Where did he pick it up?' And the old Boer waved his hand, and said: 'Over the Kopje, there, beyond the river. How should I know, brother?—a stone is a stone!' So Ray said: 'You let me take this stone away with me!' And the old Boer went on smokin', and he said: 'One stone's the same as another. Take it, brother!' And Ray said: 'If it's what I think, I'll give you half the price I get for it.'

"The old Boer smiled, and said: 'That's all right, brother; take it, take it!'

"The next morning Ray left this old Boer, and, when he was going, he said to him: 'Well,' he said, 'I believe this is a valuable stone!' and the old Boer smiled because he knew one stone was the same as another.

"The first place Ray came to was C—, and he went to the hotel; and in the evenin' he began talkin' about the stone, and they all laughed at him, because in those days nobody had heard of diamonds in South Africa. So presently he lost his temper, and pulled out the stone and showed it round; but nobody thought it was a diamond, and they all laughed at him the more. Then one of the fellers said: 'If it's a diamond, it ought to cut glass.'

"Ray took the stone, and, by Jove, he cut his name on the window, and there it is—I've seen it—on the bar window of that hotel. Well, next day, you bet, he travelled straight back to where the old Boer told him the shepherd had picked up the stone, and he went to a native chief called Jointje, and said to him: 'Jointje,' he said, 'I go a journey. While I go, you go about and send all your "boys" about, and look for all the stones that shine like this one; and when I come back, if you find me plenty, I give you gun.' And Jointje said: 'That all right, Boss.'

"And Ray went down to Cape Town, and took the stone to a jeweller, and the jeweller told him it was a diamond of about 30 or 40 carats, and gave him five hundred pound for it. So he bought a waggon and a span of oxen to give to the old Boer, and went back to Jointje. The niggers had collected skinfuls of stones of all kinds, and out of all the skinfuls Ray found three or four diamonds. So he went to work and got another feller to back him, and between them they made the Government move. The rush began, and they found that place near Kimberley; and after that they found De Beers, and after that Kimberley itself."

Travers stopped, and looked around him.

"Ray made his fortune, I suppose?"

"No, Mr. Askew; the unfortunate feller made next to nothin'. He was one of those fellers that never do any good for themselves."

"But what has all this to do with the war?"

Again Travers looked round, and more slowly than ever, said:

"Without that game of marbles, would there have been a Moer-Klip—without the Moer-Klip, would there have been a Kimberley—without Kimberley, would there have been a Rhodes—without a Rhodes, would there have been a Raid—without a Raid, would the Boers have started armin'—if the Boers hadn't armed, would there have been a Transvaal War? And if there hadn't been the Transvaal War, would there have been the incident of those two German ships we held up; and all the general feelin' in Germany that gave the Kaiser the chance to start his Navy programme in 1900? And if the Germans hadn't built their Navy, would their heads have swelled till they challenged the world, and should we have had this war?"

He slowly drew a hand from his pocket, and put it on the table. On the little finger was blazing an enormous diamond.

"My father," he said, "bought it of the jeweller."

The mother-stone glittered and glowed, and the five Englishmen fixed their eyes on it in silence. Some of them had been in the Boer War, and three of them had sons in this. At last one of them said:

"Well, that's seeing God in a dew-drop with a vengeance. What about the old Boer?"

Travers's little eyes twinkled.

"Well," he said, "Ray told me the old feller just looked at him as if he thought he'd done a damn silly thing to give him a waggon; and he nodded his old head, and said, laughin' in his beard: 'Wish you good luck, brother, with your stone.' You couldn't humbug that old Boer; he knew one stone was the same as another."

CHAPTER XII

POIROT AND BIDAN

A RECOLLECTION

Coming one dark December evening out of the hospital courtyard into the corridor which led to my little workroom, I was conscious of two new arrivals. There were several men round the stove, but these two were sitting apart on a bench close to my door. We used to get men in all stages of decrepitude, but I had never seen two who looked so completely under the weather. They were the extremes—in age, in colouring, in figure, in everything; and they sat there, not speaking, with every appearance of apathy and exhaustion. The one was a boy, perhaps nineteen, with a sunken, hairless, grey-white face under his peaked cap—never surely was face so grey! He sat with his long grey-blue overcoat open at the knees, and his long emaciated hands nervously rubbing each other between them. Intensely forlorn he looked, and I remember thinking: "That boy's dying!" This was Bidan.

The other's face, in just the glimpse I had of it, was as if carved out of wood, except for that something you see behind the masks of driven bullocks, deeply resentful. His cap was off, and one saw he was grey-haired; his cheeks, stretched over cheekbones solid as door-handles, were a purplish-red, his grey moustache was damp, his light blue eyes stared like a codfish's. He reminded me queerly of those Parisian cochers one still sees under their shining hats, wearing an expression of being your enemy. His short stocky figure was dumped stolidly as if he meant never to move again; on his thick legs and feet he wore mufflings of cloth boot, into which his patched and stained grey-blue trousers were tucked. One of his gloved hands was stretched out stiff on his knee. This was Poirot.

Two more dissimilar creatures were never blown together into our haven. So far as I remember, they had both been in hospital about six months, and their ailments were, roughly speaking, Youth and Age. Bidan had not finished his training when his weak constitution gave way under it; Poirot was a Territorial who had dug behind the Front till rheumatism claimed him for its own. Bidan, who had fair hair and rather beautiful brown eyes over which the lids could hardly keep up, came from Aix-en-Provence, in the very south; Poirot from Nancy, in the northeast. I made their acquaintance the next morning.

The cleaning of old Poirot took, literally speaking, days to accomplish. Such an encrusted case we had never seen; nor was it possible to go, otherwise than slowly, against his prejudices. One who, unless taken exactly the right way, considered everyone leagued with Nature to get the better of him, he had reached that state when the soul sticks its toes in and refuses to budge. A coachman—in civil life—a socialist, a freethinker, a wit, he was the apex of—shall we say?—determination. His moral being was encrusted with perversity, as his poor hands and feet with dirt. Oil was the only thing for him, and I, for one, used oil on him morally and physically, for months. He was a "character!" His left hand—which he was never tired of saying the "majors" had ruined ("Ah! les cochons!") by leaving it alone—was stiff in all its joints, so that the fingers would not bend; and the little finger of the right hand, "le petit," "le coquin," "l'empereur," as he would severally call it, was embellished by chalky excrescences. The old fellow had that peculiar artfulness which comes from life-long dealing with horses, and he knew exactly how far and how quickly it was advisable for him to mend in health. About the third day he made up his mind that he wished to remain with us at least until the warm weather came. For that it would be necessary—he concluded—to make a cheering amount of progress, but not too much. And this he set himself to do. He was convinced, one could see, that after Peace had been declared and compensation assured him, he would recover the use of his hand, even if "l'empereur" remained stiff and chalky. As a matter of fact, I think he was mistaken, and will never have a supple left hand again. But his arms were so brawny, his constitution so vigorous, and his legs improved so rapidly under the necessity of taking him down into the little town for his glass, of an afternoon, that one felt he might possibly be digging again sooner than he intended.

"Ah, les cochons!" he would say; "while one finger does not move, they shall pay me!" He was very bitter against all "majors" save one, who it seemed had actually sympathised with him, and all députés, who for him constituted the powers of darkness, drawing their salaries, and sitting in their chairs. ("Ah! les chameaux!")

Though he was several years younger than oneself, one always thought of him as "Old Poirot" indeed, he was soon called "le grand-père," though no more confirmed bachelor ever inhabited the world. He was a regular "Miller of Dee," caring for nobody; and yet he was likeable, that humorous old stoic, who suffered from gall-stones, and bore horrible bouts of pain like a hero. In spite of all his disabilities his health and appearance soon became robust in our easy-going hospital, where no one was harried, the food excellent, and the air good. He would tell you that his father lived to eighty, and his grandfather to a hundred, both "strong men" though not so strong as his old master, the squire, of whose feats in the hunting-field he would give most staggering accounts in an argot which could only be followed by instinct. A great narrator, he would describe at length life in the town of Nancy, where, when the War broke out, he was driving a market cart, and distributing vegetables, which had made him an authority on municipal reform. Though an incorrigible joker, his stockfish countenance would remain perfectly grave, except for an occasional hoarse chuckle. You would have thought he had no more power of compassion than a cat, no more sensibility than a Chinese idol; but this was not so. In his wooden, shrewd, distrustful way he responded to sympathy, and was even sorry for others. I used to like very much his attitude to the young "stable-companion" who had arrived with him; he had no contempt, such as he might easily have felt for so weakly a creature, but rather a real indulgence towards his feebleness. "Ah!" he would say at first; "he won't make old bones—that one!" But he seemed extremely pleased when, in a fortnight or so, he had to modify that view, for Bidan (Prosper) prospered more rapidly even than himself. That grey look was out of the boy's face within three weeks. It was wonderful to watch him come back to life, till at last he could say, with his dreadful Provençal twang, that he felt "très biang." A most amiable youth, he had been a cook, and his chief ambition was to travel till he had attained the summit of mortal hopes, and was cooking at the Ritz in London. When he came to us his limbs seemed almost to have lost their joints, they wambled so. He had no muscle at all. Utter anæmia had hold of all his body, and all but a corner of his French spirit. Round that unquenchable gleam of gaiety the rest of him slowly rallied. With proper food and air and freedom, he began to have a faint pink flush in his china-white cheeks; his lids no longer drooped, his limbs seemed to regain their joints, his hands ceased to swell, he complained less and less of the pains about his heart. When, of a morning, he was finished with, and "le grand-père" was having his hands done, they would engage in lively repartee—oblivious of one's presence. We began to feel that this grey ghost of a youth had been well named, after all, when they called him Prosper, so lyrical would he wax over the constitution and cooking of "bouillabaisse," over the South, and the buildings of his native Aix-en-Provence. In all France you could not have found a greater contrast than those two who had come to us so under the weather; nor in all France two better instances of the way men can regain health of body and spirit in the right surroundings.

We had a tremendous fall of snow that winter, and had to dig ourselves out of it. Poirot and Bidan were of those who dug. It was amusing to watch them. Bidan dug easily, without afterthought. "Le grand-père" dug, with half an eye at least on his future; in spite of those stiff fingers he shifted a lot of snow, but he rested on his shovel whenever he thought you could see him—for he was full of human nature.

To see him and Bidan set off for town together! Bidan pale, and wambling a little still, but gay, with a kind of birdlike detachment; "le grand-père" stocky, wooden, planting his huge feet rather wide apart and regarding his companion, the frosted trees, and the whole wide world, with his humorous stare.

Once, I regret to say, when spring was beginning to come, Bidan-Prosper returned on "le grand-père's" arm with the utmost difficulty, owing to the presence within him of a liquid called Clairette de Die, no amount of which could subdue "le grand-père's" power of planting one foot before the other. Bidan-Prosper arrived hilarious, revealing to the world unsuspected passions; he awoke next morning sad, pale, penitent. Poirot, au contraire, was morose the whole evening, and awoke next morning exactly the same as usual. In such different ways does the gift of the gods affect us.

They had their habits, so diverse, their constitutions, and their dreams—alas! not yet realised. I know not where they may be now; Bidan-Prosper cannot yet be cooking at the Ritz in London town; but "grand-père" Poirot may perchance be distributing again his vegetables in the streets of Nancy, driving his two good little horses—des gaillards—with the reins hooked round "l'empereur." Good friends— good luck!

CHAPTER XIII

THE MUFFLED SHIP

It was cold and grey, but the band on shore was playing, and the flags on shore were fluttering, and the long double-tiered wharf crowded with welcomers in each of its open gaps, when our great ship slowly drew alongside, packed with cheering, chattering crowds of khaki figures, letting go all the pent-up excitement of getting home from the war. The air was full of songs and laughter, of cheers, and shouted questions, the hooting of the launches' sirens, the fluttering flags and hands and handkerchiefs; and there were faces of old women, and of girls, intent, expectant, and the white gulls were floating against the grey sky, when our ship, listed slightly by those thousands of figures straining towards the land which had bred them, gently slurred up against the high wharf, and was made fast.

The landing went on till night had long fallen, and the band was gone. At last the chatter, the words of command, the snatches of song, and that most favourite chorus: "Me! and my girl!" died away, and the wharf was silent and the ship silent, and a wonderful clear dark beauty usurped the spaces of the sky. By the light of the stars and a half moon the far harbour shores were just visible, the huddled buildings on the near shore, the spiring masts and feathery appanage of ropes on the moored ship, and one blood-red light above the black water. The night had all that breathless beauty which steeps the soul in a quivering, quiet rapture....

Then it was that clearly, as if I had been a welcomer standing on land in one of the wharf gaps, I saw her come—slow, slow, creeping up the narrow channel, in beside the wharf, a great grey silent ship. At first I thought her utterly empty, deserted, possessed only by the thick coiled cables forward, the huge rusty anchors, the piled-up machinery of structure and funnel and mast, weird in the blue darkness. A lantern on the wharf cast a bobbing golden gleam deep into the oily water at her side. Gun-grey, perfectly mute, she ceased to move, coming to rest against the wharf. And then, with a shiver, I saw that something clung round her, a grey film or emanation, which shifted and hovered, like the invisible wings of birds in a thick mist. Gradually to my straining eyes that filmy emanation granulated, and became faces attached to grey filmy forms, thousands on thousands, and every face bent towards the shore, staring, as it seemed, through me, at all that was behind me. Slowly, very slowly, I made them out—faces of helmeted soldiers, bulky with the gear of battle, their arms outstretched, and the lips of every one opened, so that I expected to hear the sound of cheering; but no sound came. Now I could see their eyes. They seemed to beseech—like the eyes of a little eager boy who asks his mother something she cannot tell him; and their outstretched hands seemed trying to reach her, lovingly, desperately trying to reach her! And those opened lips, how terribly they seemed trying to speak! "Mother! Mother Canada!" As if I had heard, I knew they were saying—those opened lips which could speak no more! "Mother! Mother Canada! Home! Home!..."

And then away down the wharf some one chanted: "Me and my girl!" And, silent as she had come, the muffled ship vanished in all her length, with those grey forms and those mute faces; and I was standing again in the bows beside a huge hawser; below me the golden gleam bobbing deep in the oily water, and above me the cold start in beauty shining.

CHAPTER XIV

HERITAGE

(AN IMPRESSION)

From that garden seat one could see the old low house of pinkish brick, with a path of queer-shaped flagstones running its length, and the tall grey chapel from which came the humming and chanting and organ drone of the Confirmation Service. But for that, and the voices of two gardeners working below us among the fruits and flowers, the July hush was complete. And suddenly one became aware of being watched.

That thin white windmill on the hill!

Away past the house, perhaps six hundred yards, it stood, ghostly, with a face like that of a dark-eyed white owl, made by the crossing of its narrow sails. With a black companion—a yew-tree cut to pyramid form, on the central point of Sussex—it was watching us, for though one must presume it built of old time by man, it looked up there against the sky, with its owl's face and its cross, like a Christo-Pagan presence.

What exactly Paganism was we shall never know; what exactly Christianism is, we are as little likely to discover; but here and there the two principles seem to dwell together in amity. For Paganism believed in the healthy and joyful body; and Christianism in the soul superior thereto. And, where we were sitting that summer day, was the home of bodies wrecked yet learning to be joyful, and of souls not above the process.

We moved from the grey-wood seat, and came on tiptoe to where house and chapel formed a courtyard. The doors were open, and we stood unseen, listening. From the centre of a square stone fountain a little bubble of water came up, and niched along one high wall a number of white pigeons were preening their feathers, silent, and almost motionless, as though attending to the Service.

The sheer emotion of church sounds will now and then steal away reason from the unbeliever, and take him drugged and dreaming. "Defend, O Lord, this Thy child!...." So it came out to us in the dream and drowse of summer, which the little bubble of water cooled.

In his robes—cardinal, and white, and violet—the good Bishop stood in full sunlight, speaking to the crippled and the air-raid children in their drilled rows under the shade of the doves' wall; and one felt far from this age, as if one had strayed back into that time when the builders of the old house laid slow brick on brick, wetting their whistles on mead, and knowing not tobacco.

And then, out by the chapel porch moved three forms in blue, with red neckties, and we were again in this new age, watching the faces of those listening children. The good Bishop was making them feel that he was happy in their presence, and that made them happy in his. For the great thing about life is the going-out of friendliness from being to being. And if a place be beautiful, and friendliness ever on the peace-path there, what more can we desire? And yet—how ironical this place of healing, this beautiful "Heritage!" Verily a heritage of our modern civilisation which makes all this healing necessary! If life were the offspring of friendliness and beauty's long companionship, there would be no crippled children, no air-raid children, none of those good fellows in blue with red ties and maimed limbs; and the colony to which the Bishop spoke, standing grey-headed in the sun, would be dissolved. Friendliness seems so natural, beauty so appropriate to this earth! But in this torn world they are as fugitives who nest together here and there. Yet stumbling by chance on their dove-cotes and fluttering happiness, one makes a little golden note, which does not fade off the tablet.

How entrancing it is to look at a number of faces never seen before—and how exasperating!—stamped coins of lives quite separate, quite different from every other; masks pallid, sunburned, smooth, or crumpled, to peep behind which one longs, as a lover looking for his lady at carnival, or a man aching at summer beauty which he cannot quite fathom and possess. If one had a thousand lives, and time to know and sympathy to understand the heart of every creature met with, one would want—a million! May life make us all intuitive, strip away self-consciousness, and give us sunshine and unknown faces!

What were they all feeling and thinking—those little cripples doing their drill on crutches; those air-raid waifs swelling their Cockney chests, rising on their toes, puffing their cheeks out in anxiety to do their best; those soldiers in their blue "slops," with a hand gone there and a leg gone here, and this and that grievous disability, all carrying on so cheerfully?

Values are queer in this world. We are accustomed to exalt those who can say "bo" to a goose; but that gift of expression which twines a halo round a lofty brow is no guarantee of goodness in the wearer. The really good are those plucky folk who plod their silent, often suffering, generally exploited ways, from birth to death, out of reach of the music of man's praise.

The first thing each child cripple makes here is a little symbolic ladder. In making it he climbs a rung on the way to his sky of self-support; and when at last he leaves this home, he steps off the top of it into the blue, and—so they say—walks there upright and undismayed, as if he had never suffered at Fate's hands. But what do he and she—for many are of the pleasant sex—think of the sky when they get there; that dusty and smoke-laden sky of the industrialism which begat them? How can they breathe in it, coming from this place of flowers and fresh air, of clean bright workshops and elegant huts, which they on crutches built for themselves?

Masters of British industry, and leaders of the men and women who slave to make its wheels go round, make a pilgrimage to this spot, and learn what foul disfigurement you have brought on the land of England these last five generations! The natural loveliness in this Heritage is no greater than the loveliness that used to be in a thousand places which you have blotted out of the book of beauty, with your smuts and wheels, your wires and welter. And to what end? To manufacture crippled children, and pale, peaky little Cockneys whose nerves are gone; (and, to be sure, the railways and motor cars which will bring you here to see them coming to life once more in sane and natural surroundings!) Blind and deaf and dumb industrialism is the accursed thing in this land and in all others.

If only we could send all our crippled soldiers to relearn life, in places such as this; if, instead of some forty or fifty, forty or fifty thousand could begin again, under the gaze of that white windmill! If they could slough off here not only those last horrors, but the dinge and drang of their upbringing in towns, where wheels go round, lights flare, streets reek, and no larks sing, save some little blinded victim in a cage. Poor William Blake:

"I will not cease from fighting, nor shall my sword sleep in my hand, Till we have built Jerusalem in England's green and pleasant land!"

A long vigil his sword is keeping, while the clock strikes every hour of the twenty-four. We have not yet even laid Jerusalem's foundation stone. Ask one of those maimed soldier boys. "I like it here. Oh, yes, it's very pleasant for a change." But he hastens to tell you that he goes in to Brighton every day to his training school, as if that saved the situation; almost surprised he seems that beauty and peace and good air are not intolerable to his town-bred soul. The towns have got us—nearly all. Not until we let beauty and the quiet voice of the fields, and the scent of clover creep again into our nerves, shall we begin to build Jerusalem and learn peacefulness once more. The countryman hates strife; it breaks his dream. And life should have its covering of dream—bird's flight, bird's song, wind in the ash-trees and the corn, tall lilies glistening, the evening shadows slanting out, the night murmuring of waters. There is no other genuine dream; without it to sweeten all, life is harsh and shrill and east-wind dry, and evil overruns her more quickly than blight be-gums the rose-tree or frost blackens fern of a cold June night. We elders are past re-making England, but our children, even these crippled children here, may yet take a hand....

We left the tinies to the last—all Montessorians, and some of them little cripples, too, but with cheeks so red that they looked as if the colour must come off. They lived in a house past the white mill, across the common; and they led us by the hand down spotless corridors into white dormitories. The smile of the prettiest little maid of them all was the last thing one saw, leaving that "Heritage" of print frocks and children's faces, of flowers and nightingales, under the lee of a group of pines, the only dark beauty in the long sunlight.

CHAPTER XV

'A GREEN HILL FAR AWAY'

Was it indeed only last March, or in another life, that I climbed this green hill on that day of dolour, the Sunday after the last great German offensive began? A beautiful sun-warmed day it was, when the wild thyme on the southern slope smelled sweet, and the distant sea was a glitter of gold. Lying on the grass, pressing my cheek to its warmth, I tried to get solace for that new dread which seemed so cruelly unnatural after four years of war-misery.

'If only it were all over!' I said to myself; 'and I could come here, and to all the lovely places I know, without this awful contraction of the heart, and this knowledge that at every tick of my watch some human body is being mangled or destroyed. Ah, if only I could! Will there never be an end?'

And now there is an end, and I am up on this green hill once more, in December sunlight, with the distant sea a glitter of gold. And there is no cramp in my heart, no miasma clinging to my senses. Peace! It is still incredible. No more to hear with the ears of the nerves the ceaseless roll of gunfire, or see with the eyes of the nerves drowning men, gaping wounds, and death. Peace, actually Peace! The war has gone on so long that many of us have forgotten the sense of outrage and amazement we had, those first days of August, 1914, when it all began. But I have not forgotten, nor ever shall.

In some of us—I think in many who could not voice it—the war has left chiefly this feeling: 'If only I could find a country where men cared less for all that they seem to care for, where they cared more for beauty, for nature, for being kindly to each other. If only I could find that green hill far away!' Of the songs of Theocritus, of the life of St. Francis, there is no more among the nations than there is of dew on grass in an east wind. If we ever thought otherwise, we are disillusioned now. Yet there is Peace again, and the souls of men fresh-murdered are not flying into our lungs with every breath we draw.

Each day this thought of Peace becomes more real and blessed. I can lie on this green hill and praise Creation that I am alive in a world of beauty. I can go to sleep up here with the coverlet of sunlight warm on my body, and not wake to that old dull misery. I can even dream with a light heart, for my fair dreams will not be spoiled by waking, and my bad dreams will be cured the moment I open my eyes. I can look up at that blue sky without seeing trailed across it a mirage of the long horror, a film picture of all the things that have been done by men to men. At last I can gaze up at it, limpid and blue, without a dogging melancholy; and I can gaze down at that far gleam of sea, knowing that there is no murk of murder on it any more.

And the flight of birds, the gulls and rooks and little brown wavering things which flit out and along the edge of the chalk-pits, is once more refreshment to me, utterly untempered. A merle is singing in a bramble thicket; the dew has not yet dried off the bramble leaves. A feather of a moon floats across the sky; the distance sends forth homely murmurs; the sun warms my cheeks. And all of this is pure joy. No hawk of dread and horror keeps swooping down and bearing off the little birds of happiness. No accusing conscience starts forth and beckons me away from pleasure. Everywhere is supreme and flawless beauty. Whether one looks at this tiny snail shell, marvellously chased and marked, a very elf's horn whose open mouth is coloured rose; or gazes down at the flat land between here and the sea, wandering under the smile of the afternoon sunlight, seeming almost to be alive, hedgeless, with its many watching trees, and silver gulls hovering above the mushroom-coloured 'ploughs,' and fields green in manifold hues; whether one muses on this little pink daisy born so out of time, or watches that valley of brown-rose-grey woods, under the drifting shadows of low-hanging chalky clouds—all is perfect, as only Nature can be perfect on a lovely day, when the mind of him who looks on her is at rest.

On this green hill I am nearer than I have been yet to realisation of the difference between war and peace. In our civilian lives hardly anything has been changed—we do not get more butter or more petrol, the garb and machinery of war still shroud us, journals still drip hate; but in our spirits there is all the difference between gradual dying and gradual recovery from sickness.

At the beginning of the war a certain artist, so one heard, shut himself away in his house and garden, taking in no newspaper, receiving no visitors, listening to no breath of the war, seeing no sight of it. So he lived, buried in his work and his flowers—I know not for how long. Was he wise, or did he suffer even more than the rest of us who shut nothing away? Can man, indeed, shut out the very quality of his firmament, or bar himself away from the general misery of his species?

This gradual recovery of the world—this slow reopening of the great flower, Life—is beautiful to feel and see. I press my hand flat and hard down on those blades of grass, then take it away, and watch them very slowly raise themselves and shake off the bruise. So it is, and will be, with us for a long time to come. The cramp of war was deep in us, as an iron frost in the earth. Of all the countless millions who have fought and nursed and written and spoken and dug and sewn and worked in a thousand other ways to help on the business of killing, hardly any have laboured in real love of war. Ironical, indeed, that perhaps the most beautiful poem written these four years, Julian Grenfell's 'Into Battle!' was in heartfelt praise of fighting! But if one could gather the deep curses breathed by man and woman upon war since the first bugle was blown, the dirge of them could not be contained in the air which wraps this earth.

And yet the 'green hill,' where dwell beauty and kindliness, is still far away. Will it ever be nearer? Men have fought even on this green hill where I am lying. By the rampart markings on its chalk and grass, it has surely served for an encampment. The beauty of day and night, the lark's song, the sweet-scented growing things, the rapture of health, and of pure air, the majesty of the stars, and the gladness of sunlight, of song and dance and simple friendliness, have never been enough for men. We crave our turbulent fate. Can wars, then, ever cease? Look in men's faces, read their writings, and beneath masks and hypocrisies note the restless creeping of the tiger spirit! There has never been anything to prevent the millennium except the nature of the human being. There are not enough lovers of beauty among men. It all comes back to that. Not enough who want the green hill far away—who naturally hate disharmony, and the greed, ugliness, restlessness, cruelty, which are its parents and its children.

Will there ever be more lovers of beauty in proportion to those who are indifferent to beauty? Who shall answer that question? Yet on the answer depends peace. Men may have a mint of sterling qualities—be vigorous, adventurous, brave, upright, and self-sacrificing; be preachers and teachers; keen, cool-headed, just, industrious—if they have not the love of beauty, they will still be making wars. Man is a fighting animal, with sense of the ridiculous enough to know that he is a fool to fight, but not sense of the sublime enough to stop him. Ah, well! we have peace!

It is happiness greater than I have known for four years and four months, to lie here and let that thought go on its wings, quiet and free as the wind stealing soft from the sea, and blessed as the sunlight on this green hill.

PART II

OF PEACE-TIME

CHAPTER I

SPINDLEBERRIES

The celebrated painter Scudamore—whose studies of Nature had been hung on the line for so many years that he had forgotten the days when, not yet in the Scudamore manner, they depended from the sky—stood where his cousin had left him so abruptly. His lips, between comely grey moustache and comely pointed beard, wore a mortified smile, and he gazed rather dazedly at the spindleberries fallen on to the flagged courtyard from the branch she had brought to show him. Why had she thrown up her head as if he had struck her, and whisked round so that those dull-pink berries quivered and lost their rain-drops, and four had fallen? He had but said: "Charming! I'd like to use them!" And she had answered: "God!" and rushed away. Alicia really was crazed; who would have thought that once she had been so adorable! He stooped and picked up the four berries—a beautiful colour, that dull pink! And from below the coatings of success and the Scudamore manner a little thrill came up; the stir of emotional vision. Paint! What good! How express? He went across to the low wall which divided the courtyard of his expensively restored and beautiful old house from the first flood of the River Arun wandering silvery in pale winter sunlight. Yes, indeed! How express Nature, its translucence and mysterious unities, its mood never the same from hour to hour! Those brown-tufted rushes over there against the gold grey of light and water—those restless hovering white gulls! A kind of disgust at his own celebrated manner welled up within him—the disgust akin to Alicia's "God!" Beauty! What use—how express it! Had she been thinking the same thing?

He looked at the four pink berries glistening on the grey stone of the wall, and memory stirred. What a lovely girl she had been with her grey-green eyes, shining under long lashes, the rose-petal colour in her cheeks and the too-fine dark hair—now so very grey—always blowing a little wild. An enchanting, enthusiastic creature! He remembered, as if it had been but last week, that day when they started from Arundel station by the road to Burpham, when he was twenty-nine and she twenty-five, both of them painters and neither of them famed—a day of showers and sunlight in the middle of March, and Nature preparing for full Spring! How they had chattered at first; and when their arms touched, how he had thrilled, and the colour had deepened in her wet cheeks; and then, gradually, they had grown silent; a wonderful walk, which seemed leading so surely to a more wonderful end. They had wandered round through the village and down, past the chalk-pit and Jacob's ladder, onto the field path and so to the river-bank. And he had taken her ever so gently round the waist, still silent, waiting for that moment when his heart would leap out of him in words and hers—he was sure—would leap to meet it. The path entered a thicket of blackthorn, with a few primroses close to the little river running full and gentle. The last drops of a shower were falling, but the sun had burst through, and the sky above the thicket was cleared to the blue of speedwell flowers. Suddenly she had stopped and cried: "Look, Dick! Oh, look! It's heaven!" A high bush of blackthorn was lifted there, starry white against the blue and that bright cloud. It seemed to sing, it was so lovely; the whole of Spring was in it. But the sight of her ecstatic face had broken down all his restraint; and tightening his arm round her, he had kissed her lips. He remembered still the expression of her face, like a child's startled out of sleep. She had gone rigid, gasped, started away from him; quivered and gulped, and broken suddenly into sobs. Then, slipping from his arm, she had fled. He had stood at first, amazed and hurt, utterly bewildered; then, recovering a little, had hunted for her full half an hour before at last he found her sitting on wet grass, with a stony look on her face. He had said nothing, and she nothing, except to murmur: "Let's go on; we shall miss our train!" And all the rest of that day and the day after, until they parted, he had suffered from the feeling of having tumbled down off some high perch in her estimation. He had not liked it at all; it had made him very angry. Never from that day to this had he thought of it as anything but a piece of wanton prudery. Had it—had it been something else?

He looked at the four pink berries, and, as if they had uncanny power to turn the wheel of memory, he saw another vision of his cousin five years later. He was married by then, and already hung on the line. With his wife he had gone down to Alicia's country cottage. A summer night, just dark and very warm. After many exhortations she had brought into the little drawing-room her last finished picture. He could see her now placing it where the light fell, her tall slight form already rather sharp and meagre, as the figures of some women grow at thirty, if they are not married; the nervous, fluttering look on her charming face, as though she could hardly bear this inspection; the way she raised her shoulder just a little as if to ward off an expected blow of condemnation. No need! It had been a beautiful thing, a quite surprisingly beautiful study of night. He remembered with what a really jealous ache he had gazed at it—a better thing than he had ever done himself. And, frankly, he had said so. Her eyes had shone with pleasure.

"Do you really like it? I tried so hard!"

"The day you show that, my dear," he had said, "your name's made!" She had clasped her hands and simply sighed: "Oh, Dick!" He had felt quite happy in her happiness, and presently the three of them had taken their chairs out, beyond the curtains, on to the dark verandah, had talked a little, then somehow fallen silent. A wonderful warm, black, grape-bloom night, exquisitely gracious and inviting; the stars very high and white, the flowers glimmering in the garden-beds, and against the deep, dark blue, roses hanging, unearthly, stained with beauty. There was a scent of honeysuckle, he remembered, and many moths came fluttering by towards the tall narrow chink of light between the curtains. Alicia had sat leaning forward, elbows on knees, ears buried in her hands. Probably they were silent because she sat like that. Once he heard her whisper to herself: "Lovely, lovely! Oh, God! How lovely!" His wife, feeling the dew, had gone in, and he had followed; Alicia had not seemed to notice. But when she too came in, her eyes were glistening with tears. She said something about bed in a queer voice; they had taken candles and gone up. Next morning, going to her little studio to give her advice about that picture, he had been literally horrified to see it streaked with lines of Chinese white—Alicia, standing before it, was dashing her brush in broad smears across and across. She heard him and turned round. There was a hard red spot in either cheek, and she said in a quivering voice: "It was blasphemy. That's all!" And turning her back on him, she had gone on smearing it with Chinese white. Without a word, he had turned tail in simple disgust. Indeed, so deep had been his vexation at that wanton destruction of the best thing she had ever done, or was ever likely to do, that he had avoided her for years. He had always had a horror of eccentricity. To have planted her foot firmly on the ladder of fame and then deliberately kicked it away; to have wantonly foregone this chance of making money—for she had but a mere pittance! It had seemed to him really too exasperating, a thing only to be explained by tapping one's forehead. Every now and then he still heard of her, living down there, spending her days out in the woods and fields, and sometimes even her nights, they said, and steadily growing poorer and thinner and more eccentric; becoming, in short, impossibly difficult, as only Englishwomen can. People would speak of her as "such a dear," and talk of her charm, but always with that shrug which is hard to bear when applied to one's relations. What she did with the productions of her brush he never inquired, too disillusioned by that experience. Poor Alicia!

The pink berries glowed on the grey stone, and he had yet another memory. A family occasion when Uncle Martin Scudamore departed this life, and they all went up to bury him and hear his Will. The old chap, whom they had looked on as a bit of a disgrace, money-grubbing up in the little grey Yorkshire town which owed its rise to his factory, was expected to make amends by his death, for he had never married—too sunk in Industry, apparently, to have the time. By tacit agreement, his nephews and nieces had selected the Inn at Bolton Abbey, nearest beauty spot, for their stay. They had driven six miles to the funeral in three carriages. Alicia had gone with him and his brother, the solicitor. In her plain black clothes she looked quite charming, in spite of the silver threads already thick in her fine dark hair, loosened by the moor wind. She had talked of painting to him with all her old enthusiasm, and her eyes had seemed to linger on his face as if she still had a little weakness for him. He had quite enjoyed that drive. They had come rather abruptly on the small grimy town clinging to the river-banks, with old Martin's long yellow-brick house dominating it, about two hundred yards above the mills. Suddenly under the rug he felt Alicia's hand seize his with a sort of desperation, for all the world as if she were clinging to something to support her. Indeed, he was sure she did not know it was his hand she squeezed. The cobbled streets, the muddy-looking water, the dingy, staring factories, the yellow staring house, the little dark-clothed, dreadfully plain work-people, all turned out to do a last honour to their creator; the hideous new grey church, the dismal service, the brand-new tombstones—and all of a glorious autumn day! It was inexpressibly sordid—too ugly for words! Afterwards the Will was read to them, seated decorously on bright mahogany chairs in the yellow mansion; a very satisfactory Will, distributing in perfectly adjusted portions, to his own kinsfolk and nobody else, a very considerable wealth. Scudamore had listened to it dreamily, with his eyes fixed on an oily picture, thinking: "My God! What a thing!" and longing to be back in the carriage smoking a cigar to take the reek of black clothes, and sherry—sherry!—out of his nostrils. He happened to look at Alicia. Her eyes were closed; her lips, always sweet-looking, quivered amusedly. And at that very moment the Will came to her name. He saw those eyes open wide, and marked a beautiful pink flush, quite like that of old days, come into her thin cheeks. "Splendid!" he had thought; "it's really jolly for her. I am glad. Now she won't have to pinch. Splendid!" He shared with her to the full the surprised relief showing in her still beautiful face.

All the way home in the carriage he felt at least as happy over her good fortune as over his own, which had been substantial. He took her hand under the rug and squeezed it, and she answered with a long, gentle pressure, quite unlike the clutch when they were driving in. That same evening he strolled out to where the river curved below the Abbey. The sun had not quite set, and its last smoky radiance slanted into the burnished autumn woods. Some white-faced Herefords were grazing in lush grass, the river rippled and gleamed, all over golden scales. About that scene was the magic which has so often startled the hearts of painters, the wistful gold—the enchantment of a dream. For some minutes he had gazed with delight which had in it a sort of despair. A little crisp rustle ran along the bushes; the leaves fluttered, then hung quite still. And he heard a voice—Alicia's—speaking. "My lovely, lovely world!" And moving forward a step, he saw her standing on the river-bank, braced against the trunk of a birch-tree, her head thrown back, and her arms stretched wide apart as though to clasp the lovely world she had apostrophised. To have gone up to her would have been like breaking up a lovers' interview, and he turned round instead and went away.

A week later he heard from his brother that Alicia had refused her legacy. "I don't want it," her letter had said simply, "I couldn't bear to take it. Give it to those poor people who live in that awful place." Really eccentricity could go no further! They decided to go down and see her. Such mad neglect of her own good must not be permitted without some effort to prevent it. They found her very thin, and charming; humble, but quite obstinate in her refusal. "Oh! I couldn't, really! I should be so unhappy. Those poor little stunted people who made it all for him! That little, awful town! I simply couldn't be reminded. Don't talk about it, please. I'm quite all right as I am." They had threatened her with lurid pictures of the workhouse and a destitute old age. To no purpose, she would not take the money. She had been forty when she refused that aid from heaven—forty, and already past any hope of marriage. For though Scudamore had never known for certain that she had ever wished or hoped for marriage, he had his theory—that all her eccentricity came from wasted sexual instinct. This last folly had seemed to him monstrous enough to be pathetic, and he no longer avoided her. Indeed, he would often walk over to tea in her little hermitage. With Uncle Martin's money he had bought and restored the beautiful old house over the River Arun, and was now only five miles from Alicia's across country. She too would come tramping over at all hours, floating in with wild flowers or ferns, which she would put into water the moment she arrived. She had ceased to wear hats, and had by now a very doubtful reputation for sanity about the countryside. This was the period when Watts was on every painter's tongue, and he seldom saw Alicia without a disputation concerning that famous symbolist. Personally, he had no use for Watts, resenting his faulty drawing and crude allegories, but Alicia always maintained with her extravagant fervour that he was great because he tried to paint the soul of things. She especially loved a painting called "Iris"—a female symbol of the rainbow, which indeed in its floating eccentricity had a certain resemblance to herself. "Of course he failed," she would say; "he tried for the impossible and went on trying all his life. Oh! I can't bear your rules, and catchwords, Dick; what's the good of them! Beauty's too big, too deep!" Poor Alicia! She was sometimes very wearing.

He never knew quite how it came about that she went abroad with them to Dauphiné in the autumn of 1904—a rather disastrous business—never again would he take anyone travelling who did not know how to come in out of the cold. It was a painter's country, and he had hired a little chateau in front of the Glandaz mountain—himself, his wife, their eldest girl, and Alicia. The adaptation of his famous manner to that strange scenery, its browns and French greys and filmy blues, so preoccupied him that he had scant time for becoming intimate with these hills and valleys. From the little gravelled terrace in front of the annex, out of which he had made a studio, there was an absorbing view over the pan-tiled old town of Die. It glistened below in the early or late sunlight, flat-roofed and of pinkish-yellow, with the dim, blue River Drôme circling one side, and cut, dark cypress-trees dotting the vineyarded slopes. And he painted it continually. What Alicia did with herself they none of them very much knew, except that she would come in and talk ecstatically of things and beasts and people she had seen. One favourite haunt of hers they did visit, a ruined monastery high up in the amphitheatre of the Glandaz mountain. They had their lunch up there, a very charming and remote spot, where the watercourses and ponds and chapel of the old monks were still visible, though converted by the farmer to his use. Alicia left them abruptly in the middle of their praises, and they had not seen her again till they found her at home when they got back. It was almost as if she had resented laudation of her favourite haunt. She had brought in with her a great bunch of golden berries, of which none of them knew the name; berries almost as beautiful as these spindleberries glowing on the stone of the wall. And a fourth memory of Alicia came.

Christmas Eve, a sparkling frost, and every tree round the little chateau rimed so that they shone in the starlight, as though dowered with cherry blossoms. Never were more stars in clear black sky above the whitened earth. Down in the little town a few faint points of yellow light twinkled in the mountain wind, keen as a razor's edge. A fantastically lovely night—quite "Japanese," but cruelly cold. Five minutes on the terrace had been enough for all of them except Alicia. She—unaccountable, crazy creature—would not come in. Twice he had gone out to her, with commands, entreaties, and extra wraps; the third time he could not find her, she had deliberately avoided his onslaught and slid off somewhere to keep this mad vigil by frozen starlight. When at last she did come in she reeled as if drunk. They tried to make her really drunk, to put warmth back into her. No good! In two days she was down with double pneumonia; it was two months before she was up again—a very shadow of herself. There had never been much health in her since then. She floated like a ghost through life, a crazy ghost, who still would steal away, goodness knew where, and come in with a flush in her withered cheeks, and her grey hair wild blown, carrying her spoil—some flower, some leaf, some tiny bird, or little soft rabbit. She never painted now, never even talked of it. They had made her give up her cottage and come to live with them, literally afraid that she would starve herself to death in her forgetfulness of everything. These spindleberries even! Why, probably she had been right up this morning to that sunny chalk-pit in the lew of the Downs to get them, seven miles there and back, when you wouldn't think she could walk seven hundred yards, and as likely as not had lain there on the dewy grass, looking up at the sky, as he had come on her sometimes. Poor Alicia! And once he had been within an ace of marrying her! A life spoiled! By what, if not by love of beauty! But who would have ever thought that the intangible could wreck a woman, deprive her of love, marriage, motherhood, of fame, of wealth, of health! And yet—by George!—it had!

Scudamore flipped the four pink berries off the wall. The radiance and the meandering milky waters; that swan against the brown tufted rushes; those far, filmy Downs—there was beauty! Beauty! But, damn it all—moderation! And, turning his back on that prospect, which he had painted so many times, in his celebrated manner, he went in, and up the expensively restored staircase to his studio. It had great windows on three sides, and perfect means for regulating light. Unfinished studies melted into walls so subdued that they looked like atmosphere. There were no completed pictures— they sold too fast. As he walked over to his easel, his eye was caught by a spray of colour—the branch of spindleberries set in water, ready for him to use, just where the pale sunlight fell, so that their delicate colour might glow and the few tiny drops of moisture still clinging to them shine. For a second he saw Alicia herself as she must have looked, setting them there, her transparent hands hovering, her eyes shining, that grey hair of hers all fine and loose. The vision vanished! But what had made her bring them after that horrified "God!" when he spoke of using them? Was it her way of saying: "Forgive me for being rude!" Really she was pathetic, that poor devotee! The spindleberries glowed in their silver-lustre jug, sprayed up against the sunlight. They looked triumphant—as well they might, who stood for that which had ruined—or, was it, saved?—a life! Alicia! She had made a pretty mess of it, and yet who knew what secret raptures she had felt with her subtle lover, Beauty, by starlight and sunlight and moonlight, in the fields and woods, on the hilltops, and by riverside! Flowers, and the flight of birds, and the ripple of the wind, and all the shifting play of light and colour which made a man despair when he wanted to use them; she had taken them, hugged them to her with no afterthought, and been happy! Who could say that she had missed the prize of life? Who could say it?... Spindleberries! A bunch of spindleberries to set such doubts astir in him! Why, what was beauty but just the extra value which certain forms and colours, blended, gave to things—just the extra value in the human market! Nothing else on earth, nothing! And the spindleberries glowed against the sunlight, delicate, remote!

Taking his palette, he mixed crimson lake, white, and ultramarine. What was that? Who sighed, away out there behind him? Nothing!

"Damn it all!" he thought; "this is childish. This is as bad as Alicia!" And he set to work to paint in his celebrated manner—spindleberries.

CHAPTER II

EXPECTATIONS

Not many years ago a couple were living in the South of England whose name was Wotchett—Ralph and Eileen Wotchett; a curious name, derived, Ralph asserted, from a Saxon Thegn called Otchar mentioned in Domesday, or at all events—when search of the book had proved vain—on the edge of that substantial record.

He—possibly the thirtieth descendant of the Thegn—was close on six feet in height and thin, with thirsty eyes, and a smile which had fixed itself in his cheeks, so on the verge of appearing was it. His hair waved, and was of a dusty shade bordering on grey. His wife, of the same age and nearly the same height as himself, was of sanguine colouring and a Cornish family, which had held land in such a manner that it had nearly melted in their grasp. All that had come to Eileen was a reversion, on the mortgageable value of which she and Ralph had been living for some time. Ralph Wotchett also had expectations. By profession he was an architect, but perhaps because of his expectations, he had always had bad luck. The involutions of the reasons why his clients died, became insolvent, abandoned their projects, or otherwise failed to come up to the scratch were followed by him alone in the full of their maze-like windings. The house they inhabited, indeed, was one of those he had designed for a client, but the 'fat chough' had refused to go into it for some unaccountable reason; he and Eileen were only perching there, however, on the edge of settling down in some more permanent house when they came into their expectations.

Considering the vicissitudes and disappointments of their life together, it was remarkable how certain they remained that they would at last cross the bar and reach the harbour of comfortable circumstance. They had, one may suppose, expectations in their blood. The germ of getting 'something for nothing' had infected their systems, so that, though they were not selfish or greedy people, and well knew how to rough it, they dreamed so of what they had not, that they continually got rid of what they had in order to obtain more of it. If for example Ralph received an order, he felt so strongly that this was the chance of his life if properly grasped, that he would almost as a matter of course increase and complicate the project till it became unworkable, or in his zeal omit some vital calculation such as a rise in the price of bricks; nor would anyone be more surprised than he at this, or more certain that all connected with the matter had been 'fat choughs' except—himself. On such occasions Eileen would get angry, but if anyone suggested that Ralph had overreached himself, she would get still angrier. She was very loyal, and fortunately rather flyaway both in mind and body; before long she always joined him in his feeling that the whole transaction had been just the usual 'skin-game' on the part of Providence to keep them out of their expectations. It was the same in domestic life. If Ralph had to eat a breakfast, which would be almost every morning, he had so many and such imaginative ways of getting from it a better breakfast than was in it, that he often remained on the edge of it, as it were. He had special methods of cooking, so as to extract from everything a more than ordinary flavour, and these took all the time that he would have to eat the results in. Coffee he would make with a whole egg, shell and all, stirred in; it had to be left on the hob for an incomparable time, and he would start to catch his train with his first cup in his hand; Eileen would have to run after him and take it away. They were, in fact, rather like a kitten which knows it has a tail, and will fly round and round all day with the expectation of catching that desirable appendage. Sometimes indeed, by sheer perseverance, of which he had a great deal in a roundabout way, Ralph would achieve something, but, when this happened, something else, not foreseen by him, had always happened first, which rendered that accomplishment nugatory and left it expensive on his hands. Nevertheless they retained their faith that some day they would get ahead of Providence and come into their own.

In view of not yet having come into their expectations they had waited to have children; but two had rather unexpectedly been born. The babes had succumbed, however, one to preparation for betterment too ingenious to be fulfilled, the other to fulfilment, itself, a special kind of food having been treated so ingeniously that it had undoubtedly engendered poison. And they remained childless.

They were about fifty when Ralph received one morning a solicitor's letter announcing the death of his godmother, Aunt Lispeth. When he read out the news they looked at their plates a full minute without speaking. Their expectations had matured. At last they were to come into something in return for nothing. Aunt Lispeth, who had latterly lived at Ipswich in a house which he had just not built for her, was an old maid. They had often discussed what she would leave them—though in no mean or grasping spirit, for they did not grudge the 'poor old girl' her few remaining years, however they might feel that she was long past enjoying herself. The chance would come to them some time, and when it did of course must be made the best of. Then Eileen said:

"You must go down at once, Ralph!"

Donning black, Ralph set off hurriedly, and just missed his train; he caught one, however, in the afternoon, and arrived that evening in Ipswich. It was October, drizzling and dark; the last cab moved out as he tried to enter it, for he had been detained by his ticket which he had put for extra readiness in his glove, and forgotten—as if the ticket collector couldn't have seen it there, the 'fat chough!' He walked up to his Aunt's house, and was admitted to a mansion where a dinner-party was going on. It was impossible to persuade the servant that this was his Aunt's, so he was obliged to retire to a hotel and wire to Eileen to send him the right address—the 'fat choughs' in the street did not seem to know it. He got her answer the following midday, and going to the proper number, found the darkened house. The two servants who admitted him described the manner of their mistress's death, and showed him up into her room. Aunt Lispeth had been laid out daintily. Ralph contemplated her with the smile which never moved from his cheeks, and with a sort of awe in his thirsty eyes. The poor old girl! How thin, how white! It had been time she went! A little stiffened twist in her neck, where her lean head had fallen to one side at the last, had not been set quite straight; and there seemed the ghost of an expression on her face, almost cynical; by looking closer he saw that it came from a gap in the white lashes of one eye, giving it an air of not being quite closed, as though she were trying to wink at him. He went out rather hastily, and ascertaining that the funeral was fixed for noon next day, paid a visit to the solicitor.

There he was told that the lawyer himself was sole executor, and he—Ralph—residuary legatee. He could not help a feeling of exultation, for he and Eileen were at that time particularly hard pressed. He restrained it, however, and went to his hotel to write to her. He received a telegram in answer next morning at ten o'clock: 'For goodness' sake leave all details to lawyer, Eileen,' which he thought very peculiar. He lunched with the lawyer after the funeral, and they opened his Aunt's will. It was quite short and simple, made certain specific bequests of lace and jewellery, left a hundred pounds to her executor the lawyer, and the rest of her property to her nephew Ralph Wotchett. The lawyer proposed to advertise for debts in the usual way, and Ralph with considerable control confined himself to urging all speed in the application for Probate, and disposal of the estate. He caught a late train back to Eileen. She received his account distrustfully; she was sure he had put his finger in the pie, and if he had it would all go wrong. Well, if he hadn't, he soon would! It was really as if loyalty had given way in her now that their expectations were on the point of being realised.

They had often discussed his Aunt's income, but they went into it again that night, to see whether it could not by fresh investment be increased. It was derived from Norwich and Birmingham Corporation Stocks, and Ralph proved that by going into industrial concerns the four hundred a year could quite safely be made into six. Eileen agreed that this would be a good thing to do, but nothing definite was decided. Now that they had come into money they did not feel so inclined to move their residence, though both felt that they might increase their scale of living, which had lately been at a distressingly low ebb. They spoke, too, about the advisability of a small car. Ralph knew of one—a second-hand Ford—to be had for a song. They ought not—he thought—to miss the chance. He would take occasion to meet the owner casually and throw out a feeler. It would not do to let the fellow know that there was any money coming to them, or he would put the price up for a certainty. In fact it would be better to secure the car before the news got about. He secured it a few days later for eighty pounds, including repairs, which would take about a month. A letter from the lawyer next day informed them that he was attending to matters with all speed; and the next five weeks passed in slowly realising that at last they had turned the corner of their lives, and were in smooth water. They ordered among other things the materials for a fowl-house long desired, which Ralph helped to put up; and a considerable number of fowls, for feeding which he had a design which would enable them to lay a great many more eggs in the future than could reasonably be expected from the amount of food put into the fowls. He also caused an old stable to be converted into a garage. He still went to London two or three times a week, to attend to business, which was not, as a rule, there. On his way from St. Pancras to Red Lion Square, where his office was, he had long been attracted by an emerald pendant with pearl clasp, in a jeweller's shop window. He went in now to ask its price. Fifty-eight pounds—emeralds were a rising market. The expression rankled in him, and going to Hatton Garden to enquire into its truth, he found the statement confirmed. 'The chief advantage of having money,' he thought, 'is to be able to buy at the right moment.' He had not given Eileen anything for a long time, and this was an occasion which could hardly be passed over. He bought the pendant on his way back to St. Pancras, the draft in payment absorbing practically all his balance. Eileen was delighted with it. They spent that evening in the nearest approach to festivity that they had known for several years. It was, as it were, the crown of the long waiting for something out of nothing. All those little acerbities which creep into the manner of two married people who are always trying to round the corner fell away, and they sat together in one large chair, talking and laughing over the countless tricks which Providence—that 'fat chough'—had played them. They carried their light-heartedness to bed.

They were awakened next morning by the sound of a car. The Ford was being delivered with a request for payment. Ralph did not pay; it would be 'all right' he said. He stabled the car, and wrote to the lawyer that he would be glad to have news, and an advance of £100. On his return from town in the evening two days later he found Eileen in the dining-room with her hair wild and an opened letter before her. She looked up with the word: "Here!" and Ralph took the letter:

Lodgers & Wayburn, Solicitors, Ipswich

Dear Mr. Wotchett,

In answer to yours of the fifteenth, I have obtained Probate, paid all debts, and distributed the various legacies. The sale of furniture took place last Monday. I now have pleasure in enclosing you a complete and I think final account, by which you will see that there is a sum in hand of £43 due to you as residuary legatee. I am afraid this will seem a disappointing result, but as you were doubtless aware (though I was not when I had the pleasure of seeing you), the greater part of your Aunt's property passed under a Deed of Settlement, and it seems she had been dipping heavily into the capital of the remainder for some years past.

Believe me,
Faithfully yours,
EDWARD LODGERS.

For a minute the only sounds were the snapping of Ralph's jaws, and Eileen's rapid breathing. Then she said:

"You never said a word about a Settlement. I suppose you got it muddled as usual!"

Ralph did not answer, too deep in his anger with the old woman who had left that 'fat chough' a hundred pounds to provide him—Ralph—with forty-three.

"You always believe what you want to believe!" cried Eileen; "I never saw such a man."

Ralph went to Ipswich on the morrow. After going into everything with the lawyer, he succeeded in varying the account by fifteen shillings, considerably more than which was absorbed by the fee for this interview, his fare, and hotel bill. The conduct of his Aunt, in having caused him to get it into his head that there was no Settlement, and in living on her capital, gave him pain quite beyond the power of expression; and more than once he recalled with a shudder that slightly quizzical look on her dead face. He returned to Eileen the following day, with his brain racing round and round. Getting up next morning, he said:

"I believe I can get a hundred for that car; I'll go up and see about it."

"Take this too," said Eileen, handing him the emerald pendant. Ralph took it with a grunt.

"Lucky," he muttered, "emeralds are a rising market. I bought it on purpose."

He came back that night more cheerful. He had sold the car for £65, and the pendant for £42—a good price, for emeralds were now on the fall! With the cheque for £43, which represented his expectations, he proved that they would only be £14 out on the whole business when the fowls and fowl-house had been paid for; and they would have the fowls—the price of eggs was going up. Eileen agreed that it was the moment to develop poultry-keeping. They might expect good returns. And holding up her face, she said:

"Give me a kiss, dear Ralph?"

Ralph gave it, with his thirsty eyes fixed, expectant, on something round the corner of her head, and the smile, which never moved, on his cheeks.

After all there was her reversion! They would come into it some day.

CHAPTER III

MANNA

I

The Petty Sessions court at Linstowe was crowded. Miracles do not happen every day, nor are rectors frequently charged with larceny. The interest roused would have relieved all those who doubt the vitality of our ancient Church. People who never went outside their farms or plots of garden, had walked as much as three miles to see the show. Mrs. Gloyn, the sandy-haired little keeper of the shop where soap and herrings, cheese, matches, boot-laces, bulls'-eyes, and the other luxuries of a countryside could be procured, remarked to Mrs. Redland, the farmer's wife, "Tis quite a gatherin' like.' To which Mrs. Redland replied, "Most like Church of a Sunday.'

More women, it is true, than men, were present, because of their greater piety, and because most of them had parted with pounds of butter, chickens, ducks, potatoes, or some such offertory in kind during the past two years, at the instance of the rector. They had a vested interest in this matter, and were present, accompanied by their grief at value unreceived. From Trover, their little village on the top of the hill two miles from Linstowe, with the squat church-tower, beautifully untouched, and ruined by the perfect restoration of the body of the building, they had trooped in; some even coming from the shore of the Atlantic, a mile beyond, across the downs, whence other upland square church-towers could be viewed on the sky-line against the grey January heavens. The occasion was in a sense unique, and its piquancy strengthened by that rivalry which is the essence of religion.

For there was no love lost between Church and Chapel in Trover, and the rector's flock had long been fortified in their power of 'parting' by fear lest 'Chapel' (also present that day in court) should mock at his impecuniousness. Not that his flock approved of his poverty. It had seemed 'silly-like' ever since the news had spread that his difficulties had been caused by a faith in shares. To improve a secure if moderate position by speculation, would not have seemed wrong, if he had not failed instead, and made himself dependent on their butter, their potatoes, their eggs and chickens. In that parish, as in others, the saying 'Nothing succeeds like success' was true, nor had the villagers any abnormal disposition to question the title-deeds of affluence.

But it is equally true that nothing irritates so much as finding that one of whom you have the right to beg is begging of you. This was why the rector's tall, thin, black figure, down which a ramrod surely had been passed at birth; his narrow, hairless, white and wasted face, with red eyebrows over eyes that seemed now burning and now melting; his grizzled red hair under a hat almost green with age; his abrupt and dictatorial voice; his abrupt and mirthless laugh—all were on their nerves. His barked-out utterances, 'I want a pound of butter—pay you Monday!' 'I want some potatoes—pay you soon!' had sounded too often in the ears of those who had found his repayments so far purely spiritual. Now and then one of the more cynical would remark, 'Ah! I told un my butter was all to market.' Or, 'The man can't 'ave no principles—he didn't get no chicken out o' me.' And yet it was impossible to let him and his old mother die on them—it would give too much pleasure 'over the way.' And they never dreamed of losing him in any other manner, because they knew his living had been purchased. Money had passed in that transaction; the whole fabric of the Church and of Society was involved. His professional conduct, too, was flawless; his sermons long and fiery; he was always ready to perform those supernumerary duties—weddings, baptisms, and burials—which yielded him what revenue he had, now that his income from the living was mortgaged up to the hilt. Their loyalty held as the loyalty of people will when some great institution of which they are members is endangered.

Gossip said that things were in a dreadful way at the Rectory; the external prosperity of that red-brick building surrounded by laurels which did not flower, heightened ironically the conditions within. The old lady, his mother, eighty years of age, was reported never to leave her bed this winter, because they had no coal. She lay there, with her three birds flying about dirtying the room, for neither she nor her son would ever let a cage-door be shut—deplorable state of things! The one servant was supposed never to be paid. The tradesmen would no longer leave goods because they could not get their money. Most of the furniture had been sold; and the dust made you sneeze 'fit to bust yourself like.'

With a little basket on his arm, the rector collected for his household three times a week, pursuing a kind of method, always in the apparent belief that he would pay on Monday, and observing the Sabbath as a day of rest. His mind seemed ever to cherish the faith that his shares were on the point of recovery; his spirit never to lose belief in his divine right to be supported. It was extremely difficult to refuse him; the postman had twice seen him standing on the railway line that ran past just below the village, 'with 'is 'at off, as if he was in two minds-like.' This vision of him close to the shining metals had powerfully impressed many good souls who loved to make flesh creep. They would say, 'I wouldn' never be surprised if something 'appened to 'im one of these days!' Others, less romantic, shook their heads, insisting that 'he wouldn' never do nothin' while his old mother lived.' Others again, more devout, maintained that 'he wouldn' never go against the Scriptures, settin' an example like that!'

II

The Petty Sessions court that morning resembled Church on the occasion of a wedding; for the villagers of Trover had put on their black clothes and grouped themselves according to their religious faiths—'Church' in the right, 'Chapel' in the left-hand aisle. They presented all that rich variety of type and monotony of costume which the remoter country still affords to the observer; their mouths were almost all a little open, and their eyes fixed with intensity on the Bench. The three magistrates—Squire Pleydell in the chair, Dr. Becket on his left, and 'the Honble' Calmady on his right—were by most seen for the first time in their judicial capacity; and curiosity was divided between their proceedings and observation of the rector's prosecutor, a small baker from the town whence the village of Trover derived its necessaries. The face of this fellow, like that of a white walrus, and the back of his bald head were of interest to everyone until the case was called, and the rector himself entered. In his thin black overcoat he advanced and stood as if a little dazed. Then, turning his ravaged face to the Bench, he jerked out:

'Good morning! Lot of people!'

A constable behind him murmured:

'Into the dock, sir, please.'

Moving across, he entered the wooden edifice.

'Quite like a pulpit,' he said, and uttered his barking laugh.

Through the court ran a stir and shuffle, as it might be of sympathy with his lost divinity, and every eye was fixed on that tall, lean figure, with the shaven face, and red, grey-streaked hair.

Entering the witness-box, the prosecutor deposed as follows:

'Last Tuesday afternoon, your Honours, I 'appened to be drivin' my cart meself up through Trover on to the cottages just above the dip, and I'd gone in to Mrs. 'Oney's, the laundress, leavin' my cart standin' same as I always do. I 'ad a bit o' gossip, an' when I come out, I see this gentleman walkin' away in front towards the village street. It so 'appens I 'appened to look in the back o' my cart, and I thinks to meself, That's funny! There's only two flat rounds—'ave I left two 'ere by mistake? I calls to Mrs. 'Oney, an' I says, "I 'aven't been absent, 'ave I, an' left ye two?" "No," she says, "only one—'ere 'tis! Why?" she says. "Well," I says, "I 'ad four when I come in to you, there's only two now. 'Tis funny!" I says. "'Ave you dropped one?" she says. "No," I says, "I counted 'em." "That's funny," she says; "perhaps a dog's 'ad it." "'E may 'ave," I says, "but the only thing I see on the road is that there." An' I pointed to this gentleman. "Oh!" she says, "that's the rector." "Yes," I says, "I ought to know that, seein' 'e's owed me money a matter of eighteen months. I think I'll drive on," I says. Well, I drove on, and come up to this gentleman. 'E turns 'is 'ead, and looks at me. "Good afternoon!" he says—like that. "Good afternoon, sir," I says. "You 'aven't seen a loaf, 'ave you?" 'E pulls the loaf out of 'is pocket. "On the ground," 'e says; "dirty," 'e says. "Do for my birds! Ha! ha!" like that. "Oh!" I says, "indeed! Now I know," I says. I kept my 'ead, but I thinks: "That's a bit too light-'earted. You owes me one pound, eight and tuppence; I've whistled for it gettin' on for two years, but you ain't content with that, it seems! Very well," I thinks; "we'll see. An' I don't give a darn whether you're a parson or not!" I charge 'im with takin' my bread.'

Passing a dirty handkerchief over his white face and huge gingery moustache, the baker was silent. Suddenly from the dock the rector called out: 'Bit of dirty bread—feed my birds. Ha, ha!'

There was a deathly little silence. Then the baker said slowly:

'What's more, I say he ate it 'imself. I call two witnesses to that.'

The Chairman, passing his hand over his hard, alert face, that of a master of hounds, asked:

'Did you see any dirt on the loaf? Be careful!'

The baker answered stolidly:

'Not a speck.'

Dr. Becket, a slight man with a short grey beard, and eyes restive from having to notice painful things, spoke.

'Had your horse moved?'

''E never moves.'

'Ha, ha!' came the rector's laugh.

The Chairman said sharply:

'Well, stand down; call the next witness.—Charles Stodder, carpenter. Very well! Go on, and tell us what you know.'

But before he could speak the rector called out in a loud voice: 'Chapel!'

'Hsssh! Sir!' But through the body of the court had passed a murmur, of challenge, as it were, from one aisle to the other.

The witness, a square man with a red face, grey hair, whiskers, and moustache, and lively excitable dark eyes, watering with anxiety, spoke in a fast soft voice:

'Tuesday afternoon, your Worships, it might be about four o'clock, I was passin' up the village, an' I saw the rector at his gate, with a loaf in 'is 'and.'

'Show us how.'

The witness held his black hat to his side, with the rounded top outwards.

'Was the loaf clean or dirty?'

Sweetening his little eyes, the witness answered:

'I should say 'twas clean.'

'Lie!'

The Chairman said sternly:

'You mustn't interrupt, sir.—You didn't see the bottom of the loaf?'

The witness's little eyes snapped.

'Not eggzactly.'

'Did the rector speak to you?'

The witness smiled. 'The rector wouldn' never stop me if I was passin'. I collects the rates.'

The rector's laugh, so like a desolate dog's bark, killed the bubble of gaiety rising in the court; and again that deathly little silence followed.

Then the Chairman said:

'Do you want to ask him anything?'

The rector turned. 'Why d' you tell lies?'

The witness screwing up his eyes, said excitedly:

'What lies 'ave I told, please?'

'You said the loaf was clean.'

'So 'twas clean, so far as I see.'

'Come to Church, and you won't tell lies.'

'Reckon I can learn truth faster in Chapel.'

The Chairman rapped his desk.

'That'll do, that'll do! Stand down! Next witness.—Emily Bleaker. Yes? What are you? Cook at the rectory? Very well. What do you know about the affair of this loaf last Tuesday afternoon?'

The witness, a broad-faced, brown-eyed girl, answered stolidly: 'Nothin', zurr.'

'Ha, ha!'

'Hssh! Did you see the loaf?'

'Noa.'

'What are you here for, then?'

'Master asked for a plate and a knaife. He an' old missus ate et for dinner. I see the plate after; there wasn't on'y crumbs on et.'

'If you never saw the loaf, how do you know they ate it?'

'Because ther' warn't nothin' else in the 'ouse.'

The rector's voice barked out:

'Quite right!'

The Chairman looked at him fixedly.

'Do you want to ask her anything?'

The rector nodded.

'You been paid your wages?'

'Noa, I 'asn't.'

'D'you know why?'

'Noa.'

'Very sorry—no money to pay you. That's all.'

This closed the prosecutor's case; and there followed a pause, during which the Bench consulted together, and the rector eyed the congregation, nodding to one here and there. Then the Chairman, turning to him, said:

'Now, sir, do you call any witnesses?'

'Yes. My bell-ringer. He's a good man. You can believe him.'

The bell-ringer, Samuel Bevis, who took his place in the witness-box, was a kind of elderly Bacchus, with permanently trembling hands. He deposed as follows:

'When I passed rector Tuesday arternoon, he calls after me: "See this!" 'e says, and up 'e held it. "Bit o' dirrty bread," 'e says; "do for my burrds." Then on he goes walkin'.'

'Did you see whether the loaf was dirty?'

'Yaas, I think 'twas dirrty.'

'Don't think! Do you know?'

'Yaas; 'twas dirrty.'

'Which side?'

'Which saide? I think 'twas dirrty on the bottom.'

'Are you sure?'

'Yaas; 'twas dirrty on the bottom, for zartain.'

'Very well. Stand down. Now, sir, will you give us your version of this matter?'

The rector, pointing at the prosecutor and the left-hand aisle, jerked out the words:

'All Chapel—want to see me down.'

The Chairman said stonily:

'Never mind that. Come to the facts, please.'

'Certainly! Out for a walk—passed the baker's cart—saw a loaf fallen in the mud—picked it up—do for my birds.'

'What birds?'

'Magpie and two starlings; quite free—never shut the cage-door; well fed.'

'The baker charges you with taking it from his cart.'

'Lie! Underneath the cart in a puddle.'

'You heard what your cook said about your eating it. Did you?'

'Yes, birds couldn't eat all—nothing in the house—Mother and I—hungry.'

'Hungry?'

'No money. Hard up—very! Often hungry. Ha, ha!'

Again through the court that queer rustle passed. The three magistrates gazed at the accused. Then 'the Honble' Calmady said:

'You say you found the loaf under the cart. Didn't it occur to you to put it back? You could see it had fallen. How else could it have come there?'

The rector's burning eyes seemed to melt.

'From the sky. Manna.' Staring round the court, he added: 'Hungry—God's elect—to the manna born!' And, throwing back his head, he laughed. It was the only sound in a silence as of the grave.

The magistrates spoke together in low tones. The rector stood motionless, gazing at them fixedly. The people in the court sat as if at a play. Then the Chairman said:

'Case dismissed.'

'Thank you.'

Jerking out that short thanksgiving, the rector descended from the dock, and passed down the centre aisle, followed by every eye.

From the Petty Sessions court the congregation wended its way back to Trover, by the muddy lane, 'Church' and 'Chapel,' arguing the case. To dim the triumph of the 'Church' the fact remained that the baker had lost his loaf and had not been compensated. The loaf was worth money; no money had passed. It was hard to be victorious and yet reduced to silence and dark looks at girding adversaries. The nearer they came to home, the more angry with 'Chapel' did they grow. Then the bell-ringer had his inspiration. Assembling his three assistants, he hurried to the belfry, and in two minutes the little old tower was belching forth the merriest and maddest peal those bells had ever furnished. Out it swung in the still air of the grey winter day, away to the very sea.

A stranger, issuing from the inn, hearing that triumphant sound, and seeing so many black-clothed people about, said to his driver:

'What is it—a wedding?'

'No, zurr, they say 'tis for the rector, like; he've a just been acquitted for larceny.'

On the Tuesday following, the rector's ravaged face and red-grey hair appeared in Mrs. Gloyn's doorway, and his voice, creaking like a saw, said:

'Can you let me have a pound of butter? Pay you soon.'

What else could he do? Not even to God's elect does the sky always send down manna.

CHAPTER IV

A STRANGE THING

Not very long ago, during a sojourn in a part of the West country never yet visited by me, I went out one fine but rather cold March morning for a long ramble. I was in one of those disillusioned moods that come to writers, bankrupt of ideas, bankrupt of confidence, a prey to that recurrent despair, the struggle with which makes the profession of the pen—as a friend once said to me—"a manly one." "Yes"—I was thinking, for all that the air was so brisk, and the sun so bright—"nothing comes to me nowadays, no flashes of light, none of those suddenly shaped visions that bring cheer and warmth to a poor devil's heart, and set his brain and pen to driving on. A bad, bad business!" And my eyes, wandering over the dip and rise, the woods, the moor, the rocks of that fine countryside, took in the loveliness thereof with the profound discontent of one who, seeing beauty, feels that he cannot render it. The high lane-banks had just been pollarded, one could see right down over the fields and gorse and bare woods tinged with that rosy brown of beech and birch twigs, and the dusty saffron of the larches. And suddenly my glance was arrested by something vivid, a sort of black and white excitement in the air. "Aha!" I thought, "a magpie. Two! Three! Good! Is it an omen?" The birds had risen at the bottom of a field, their twining, fluttering voyage—most decorative of all bird flights—was soon lost in the wood beyond, but something it had left behind in my heart; I felt more hopeful, less inclined to think about the failure of my spirit, better able to give myself up to this new country I was passing through. Over the next rise in the very winding lane I heard the sound of brisk church bells, and not three hundred yards beyond came to a village green, where knots of men dressed in the dark clothes, light ties, and bowler hats of village festivity, and of women smartened up beyond belief, were gathered, chattering, round the yard of an old, grey, square-towered church.

"What's going on?" I thought. "It's not Sunday, not the birthday of a Potentate, and surely they don't keep Saint days in this manner. It must be a wedding. Yes—there's a favour! Let's go in and see!" And, passing the expectant groups, I entered the church and made my way up the aisle. There was already a fair sprinkling of folk all turned round towards the door, and the usual licensed buzz and whisper of a wedding congregation. The church, as seems usual in remote parishes, had been built all those centuries ago to hold a population in accordance with the expectations of its tenet, "Be fruitful and multiply." But the whole population could have been seated in a quarter of its space. It was lofty and unwarmed save by excitement, and the smell of bear's-grease. There was certainly more animation than I had ever seen or savoured in a truly rural district.

The bells which had been ringing with a sort of languid joviality, fell now into the hurried crashing which marks the approach of a bride, and the people I had passed outside came thronging in. I perceived a young man—little more than a boy, who by his semi-detachment, the fumbling of his gloved hands, and the sheepishness of the smile on his good-looking, open face, was obviously the bridegroom. I liked the looks of him—a cut above the usual village bumpkin—something free and kind about his face. But no one was paying him the least attention. It was for the bride they were waiting; and I myself began to be excited. What would this young thing be like? Just the ordinary village maiden with tight cheeks, and dress; coarse veil, high colour, and eyes like a rabbit's; or something—something like that little Welsh girl on the hills whom I once passed and whose peer I have never since seen? Bending forward, I accosted an apple-faced woman in the next pew. "Can you tell me who the bride is?"

Regarding me with the grey, round, defensive glance that one bestows on strangers, she replied:

"Aw, don't 'ee know? 'Tes Gwenny Mara—prettiest, brightest maid in these parts." And, jerking her thumb towards the neglected bridegroom, she added: "He's a lucky young chap. She'm a sunny maid, for sure, and a gude maid tu."

Somehow the description did not reassure me, and I prepared for the worst.

A bubble, a stir, a rustle!

Like everyone else, I turned frankly round. She was coming up the aisle on the arm of a hard-faced, rather gipsy-looking man, dressed in a farmer's very best.

I can only tell you that to see her coming down the centre of that grey church amongst all those dark-clothed people, was like watching the dance of a sunbeam. Never had I seen a face so happy, sweet, and radiant. Smiling, eager, just lost enough to her surroundings, her hair unconquerably golden through the coarse veil; her dancing eyes clear and dark as a peat pool—she was the prettiest sight. One could only think of a young apple-tree with the spring sun on its blossom. She had that kind of infectious brightness which comes from very simple goodness. It was quite a relief to have taken a fancy to the young man's face, and to feel that she was passing into good hands.

The only flowers in the church were early daffodils, but those first children of the sun were somehow extraordinarily appropriate to the wedding of this girl. When she came out she was pelted with them, and with that miserable confetti without which not even the simplest souls can pass to bliss, it seems. There are things in life which make one feel good—sunshine, most music, all flowers, many children, some animals, clouds, mountains, bird-songs, blue sky, dancing, and here and there a young girl's face. And I had the feeling that all of us there felt good for the mere seeing of her.

When she had driven away, I found myself beside a lame old man, with whiskers, and delightful eyes, who continued to smile after the carriage had quite vanished. Noticing, perhaps, that I, too, was smiling, he said: "'Tes a funny thing, tu, when a maid like that gets married—makes you go all of a tremble—so it du." And to my nod he added: "Brave bit o' sunshine—we'll miss her hereabout; not a doubt of it. We ain't got another one like that."

"Was that her father?" I asked, for the want of something to say. With a sharpish look at my face, he shook his head.

"No, she an't got no parents, Mr. Mara bein' her uncle, as you may say. No, she an't got no parents," he repeated, and there was something ill at ease, yet juicy, about his voice, as though he knew things that he would not tell.

Since there was nothing more to wait for, I went up to the little inn, and ordered bread and cheese. The male congregation was whetting its whistle noisily within, but, as a stranger, I had the verandah to myself, and, finishing my simple lunch in the March sunlight, I paid and started on. Taking at random one of the three lanes that debouched from the bottom of the green, I meandered on between high banks, happy in the consciousness of not knowing at all where it would lead me—that essential of a country ramble. Except one cottage in a bottom and one farm on a rise, I passed nothing, nobody. The spring was late in these parts, the buds had hardly formed as yet on any trees, and now and then between the bursts of sunlight a few fine specks of snow would come drifting past me on the wind. Close to a group of pines at a high corner, the lane dipped sharply down to a long farm-house standing back in its yard, where three carts were drawn up, and an empty waggonette with its shafts in the air. And suddenly, by some broken daffodils on the seats and confetti on the ground, I perceived that I had stumbled on the bride's home, where the wedding feast was, no doubt, in progress.

Gratifying but by no means satisfying my curiosity by gazing at the lichened stone and thatch of the old house, at the pigeons, pigs, and hens at large between it and the barns, I passed on down the lane, which turned up steeply to the right beside a little stream. To my left was a long larch wood, to my right rough fields with many trees. The lane finished at a gate below the steep moorside crowned by a rocky tor. I stood there leaning on the top bar, debating whether I should ascend or no. The bracken had, most of it, been cut in the autumn, and not a hundred yards away the furze was being swaled; the little blood-red flames and the blue smoke, the yellow blossoms of the gorse, the sunlight, and some flecks of drifting snow were mingled in an amazing tangle of colour.

I had made up my mind to ascend the tor, and was pushing through the gate, when suddenly I saw a woman sitting on a stone under the wall bordering the larch wood. She was holding her head in her hands, rocking her body to and fro; and her eyes were evidently shut, for she had not noticed me. She wore a blue serge dress; her hat reposed beside her, and her dark hair was straggling about her face. That face, all blowsy and flushed, was at once wild and stupefied. A face which has been beautiful, coarsened and swollen by life and strong emotion, is a pitiful enough sight. Her dress, hat, and the way her hair had been done were redolent of the town, and of that unnameable something which clings to women whose business it is to attract men. And yet there was a gipsyish look about her, as though she had not always been of the town.

The sight of a woman's unrestrained distress in the very heart of untouched nature is so rare that one must be peculiar to remain unmoved. And there I stood, not knowing what on earth to do. She went on rocking herself to and fro, her stays creaking, and a faint moaning sound coming from her lips; and suddenly she drooped over her lap, her hands fallen to her sides, as though she had gone into a kind of coma. How go on and leave her thus; yet how intrude on what did not seem to me mere physical suffering?

In that quandary I stood and watched. This corner was quite sheltered from the wind, the sun almost hot, and the breath of the swaling reached one in the momentary calms. For three full minutes she had not moved a finger; till, beginning to think she had really fainted, I went up to her. From her drooped body came a scent of heat, and of stale violet powder, and I could see, though the east wind had outraddled them, traces of rouge on her cheeks and lips; their surface had a sort of swollen defiance, but underneath, as it were, a wasted look. Her breathing sounded faint and broken.

Mustering courage, I touched her on the arm. She raised her head and looked up. Her eyes were the best things she had left; they must have once been very beautiful. Bloodshot now from the wind, their wild, stupefied look passed after a moment into the peculiar, half-bold, half-furtive stare of women of a certain sort. She did not speak, and in my embarrassment I drew out the flask of port I always take with me on my rambles, and stammered:

"I beg your pardon—are you feeling faint? Would you care—?" And, unscrewing the top, I held out the flask. She stared at it a moment blankly, then taking it, said:

"That's kind of you. I feel to want it, tu." And, putting it to her lips, she drank, tilting back her head. Perhaps it was the tell-tale softness of her u's, perhaps the naturally strong lines of her figure thus bent back, but somehow the plumage of the town bird seemed to drop off her suddenly.

She handed back the flask, as empty as it had ever been, and said, with a hard smile:

"I dare say you thought me funny sittin' 'ere like that."

"I thought you were ill."

She laughed without the faintest mirth, and muttered:

"I did go on, didn't I?" Then, almost fiercely, added: "I got some reason, too. Seein' the old place again after all these years." Her dark eyes, which the wine seemed to have cleared and boldened, swept me up and down, taking me in, making sure perhaps whether or no she had ever seen me, and what sort of a brute I might be. Then she said: "I was born here. Are you from these parts?" I shook my head—"No, from the other side of the county."

She laughed. Then, after a moment's silence, said abruptly:

"I been to a weddin'—first I've seen since I was a girl."

Some instinct kept me silent.

"My own daughter's weddin', but nobody didn't know me—not likely."

I had dropped down under the shelter of the wall on to a stone opposite, and at those words looked at her with interest indeed. She—this coarsened, wasted, suspiciously scented woman of the town—the mother of that sweet, sunny child I had just seen married. And again instinctively silent about my own presence at the wedding, I murmured:

"I thought I saw some confetti in that farmyard as I came up the lane."

She laughed again.

"Confetti—that's the little pink and white and blue things—plenty o' that," and she added fiercely: "My own brother didn' know me—let alone my girl. How should she?—I haven't seen her since she was a baby—she was a laughin' little thing," and she gazed past me with that look in the eyes as of people who are staring back into the bygone. "I guess we was laughin' when we got her. 'Twas just here—summer-time. I 'ad the moon in my blood that night, right enough." Then, turning her eyes on my face, she added: "That's what a girl will 'ave, you know, once in a while, and like as not it'll du for her. Only thirty-five now, I am, an' pretty nigh the end o' my tether. What can you expect?—I'm a gay woman. Did for me right enough. Her father's dead, tu."

"Do you mean," I said, "because of your child?"

She nodded. "I suppose you can say that. They made me bring an order against him. He wouldn't pay up, so he went and enlisted, an' in tu years 'e was dead in the Boer War—so it killed him right enough. But there she is, a sweet sprig if ever there was one. That's a strange thing, isn't it?" And she stared straight before her in a sudden silence. Nor could I find anything to say, slowly taking in the strangeness of this thing. That girl, so like a sunbeam, of whom the people talked as though she were a blessing in their lives—her coming into life to have been the ruin of the two who gave her being!

The woman went on dully: "Funny how I knew she was goin' to be married—'twas a farmer told me—comes to me regular when he goes to Exeter market. I always knew he came from near my old home. 'There's a weddin' on Tuesday,' 'e says, 'I'd like to be the bridegroom at. Prettiest, sunniest maid you ever saw'; an' he told me where she come from, so I knew. He found me a bit funny that afternoon. But he don't know who I am, though he used to go to school with me; I'd never tell, not for worlds." She shook her head vehemently. "I don't know why I told you; I'm not meself to-day, and that's a fact." At her half-suspicious, half-appealing look, I said quickly:

"I don't know a soul about here. It's all right."

She sighed. "It was kind of you; and I feel to want to talk sometimes. Well, after he was gone, I said to myself: 'I'll take a holiday and go an' see my daughter married.'" She laughed—"I never had no pink and white and blue little things myself. That was all done up for me that night I had the moon in me blood. Ah! my father was a proper hard man. 'Twas bad enough before I had my baby; but after, when I couldn't get the father to marry me, an' he cut an' run, proper life they led me, him and stepmother.

Cry! Didn' I cry—I was a soft-hearted thing—never went to sleep with me eyes dry—never. 'Tis a cruel thing to make a young girl cry."

I said quietly: "Did you run away, then?"

She nodded. "Bravest thing I ever did. Nearly broke my 'eart to leave my baby; but 'twas that or drownin' myself. I was soft then. I went off with a young fellow—bookmaker that used to come over to the sports meetin', wild about me—but he never married me"—again she uttered her hard laugh— "knew a thing worth tu o' that." Lifting her hand towards the burning furze, she added: "I used to come up here an' help 'em light that when I was a little girl." And suddenly she began to cry. It was not so painful and alarming as her first distress, for it seemed natural now.

At the side of the cart-track by the gate was an old boot thrown away, and it served me for something to keep my eyes engaged. The dilapidated black object among the stones and wild plants on that day of strange mixed beauty was as incongruous as this unhappy woman herself revisiting her youth. And there shot into my mind a vision of this spot as it might have been that summer night when she had "the moon in her blood"—queer phrase—and those two young creatures in the tall soft fern, in the warmth and the darkened loneliness, had yielded to the impulse in their blood. A brisk fluttering of snowflakes began falling from the sky still blue, drifting away over our heads towards the blood-red flames and smoke. They powdered the woman's hair and shoulders, and with a sob and a laugh she held up her hand and began catching them as a child might.

"'Tis a funny day for my girl's weddin'," she said. Then with a sort of fierceness added: "She'll never know her mother—she's in luck there, tu!" And, grabbing her feathered hat from the ground, she got up. "I must be gettin' back for my train, else I'll be late for an appointment."

When she had put her hat on, rubbed her face, dusted and smoothed her dress, she stood looking at the burning furze. Restored to her town plumage, to her wonted bravado, she was more than ever like that old discarded boot, incongruous.

"I'm a fool ever to have come," she said; "only upset me—and you don't want no more upsettin' than you get, that's certain. Good-bye, and thank you for the drink—it lusened my tongue praaper, didn't it?" She gave me a look—not as a professional—but a human, puzzled look. "I told you my baby was a laughin' little thing. I'm glad she's still like that. I'm glad I've seen her." Her lips quivered for a second; then, with a faked jauntiness, she nodded. "So long!" and passed through the gate down into the lane.

I sat there in the snow and sunlight some minutes after she was gone. Then, getting up, I went and stood by the burning furze. The blowing flames and the blue smoke were alive and beautiful; but behind them they were leaving blackened skeleton twigs.

"Yes," I thought, "but in a week or two the little green grass-shoots will be pushing up underneath into the sun. So the world goes! Out of destruction! It's a strange thing!"

CHAPTER V

TWO LOOKS

The old Director of the 'Yew Trees' Cemetery walked slowly across from his house, to see that all was ready.

He had seen pass into the square of earth committed to his charge so many to whom he had been in the habit of nodding, so many whose faces even he had not known. To him it was the everyday event; yet this funeral, one more in the countless tale, disturbed him—a sharp reminder of the passage of time.

For twenty years had gone by since the death of Septimus Godwin, the cynical, romantic doctor who had been his greatest friend; by whose cleverness all had sworn, of whose powers of fascination all had gossiped! And now they were burying his son!

He had not seen the widow since, for she had left the town at once; but he recollected her distinctly, a tall, dark woman with bright brown eyes, much younger than her husband, and only married to him eighteen months before he died. He remembered her slim figure standing by the grave, at that long-past funeral, and the look on her face which had puzzled him so terribly—a look of—a most peculiar look!

He thought of it even now, walking along the narrow path towards his old friend's grave—the handsomest in the cemetery, commanding from the topmost point the whitened slope and river that lay beyond. He came to its little private garden. Spring flowers were blossoming; the railings had been freshly painted; and by the door of the grave wreaths awaited the new arrival. All was in order.

The old Director opened the mausoleum with his key. Below, seen through a thick glass floor, lay the shining coffin of the father; beneath, on the lower tier, would rest the coffin of the son.

A gentle voice, close behind him, said:

"Can you tell me, sir, what they are doing to my old doctor's grave?"

The old Director turned, and saw before him a lady well past middle age. He did not know her face, but it was pleasant, with faded rose-leaf cheeks, and silvered hair under a shady hat.

"Madam, there is a funeral here this afternoon."

"Ah! Can it be his wife?"

"Madam, his son; a young man of only twenty."

"His son! At what time did you say?"

"At two o'clock."

"Thank you; you are very kind."

With uplifted hat, he watched her walk away. It worried him to see a face he did not know.

All went off beautifully; but, dining that same evening with his friend, a certain doctor, the old Director asked:

"Did you see a lady with grey hair hovering about this afternoon?"

The doctor, a tall man, with a beard still yellow, drew his guest's chair nearer to the fire.

"I did."

"Did you remark her face? A very odd expression—a sort of—what shall I call it?—Very odd indeed! Who is she? I saw her at the grave this morning."

The doctor shook his head.

"Not so very odd, I think."

"Come! What do you mean by that?"

The doctor hesitated. Then, taking the decanter, he filled his old friend's glass, and answered:

"Well, sir, you were Godwin's greatest chum—I will tell you, if you like, the story of his death. You were away at the time, if you remember."

"It is safe with me," said the old Director.

"Septimus Godwin," began the doctor slowly, "died on a Thursday about three o'clock, and I was only called in to see him at two. I found him far gone, but conscious now and then. It was a case of—but you know the details, so I needn't go into that. His wife was in the room, and on the bed at his feet lay his pet dog—a terrier; you may recollect, perhaps, he had a special breed. I hadn't been there ten minutes, when a maid came in and whispered something to her mistress. Mrs. Godwin answered angrily, 'See him? Go down and say she ought to know better than to come here at such a time!' The maid went, but soon came back. Could the lady see Mrs. Godwin for just a moment? Mrs. Godwin answered that she could not leave her husband. The maid looked frightened, and went away again. She came back for the third time. The lady had said she must see Dr. Godwin; it was a matter of life and death! 'Death— indeed!' exclaimed Mrs. Godwin: 'Shameful! Go down and tell her, if she doesn't go immediately, I will send for the police!'

"The poor maid looked at me. I offered to go down and see the visitor myself. I found her in the dining room, and knew her at once. Never mind her name, but she belongs to a county family not a hundred miles from here. A beautiful woman she was then; but her face that day was quite distorted.

"'For God's sake, Doctor,' she said, 'is there any hope?'

"I was obliged to tell her there was none.

"'Then I must see him,' she said.

"I begged her to consider what she was asking. But she held me out a signet ring. Just like Godwin— wasn't it—that sort of Byronism, eh?

"'He sent me this,' she said, 'an hour ago. It was agreed between us that if ever he sent that, I must come. If it were only myself I could bear it—a woman can bear anything; but he'll die thinking I wouldn't come, thinking I didn't care—and I would give my life for him this minute!'

"Now, a dying man's request is sacred. I told her she should see him. I made her follow me upstairs, and wait outside his room. I promised to let her know if he recovered consciousness. I have never been thanked like that, before or since.

"I went back into the bedroom. He was still unconscious, and the terrier whining. In the next room a child was crying—the very same young man we buried to-day. Mrs. Godwin was still standing by the bed.

"'Have you sent her away?'

"I had to say that Godwin really wished to see her. At that she broke out:

"'I won't have her here—the wretch!'

"I begged her to control herself, and remember that her husband was a dying man.

"'But I'm his wife,' she said, and flew out of the room."

The doctor paused, staring at the fire. He shrugged his shoulders, and went on: "I'd have stopped her fury if I could! A dying man is not the same as the live animal, that he must needs be wrangled over! And suffering's sacred, even to us doctors. I could hear their voices outside. Heaven knows what they said to each other. And there lay Godwin with his white face and his black hair—deathly still—fine-looking fellow he always was! Then I saw that he was coming to! The women had begun again outside—first, the wife, sharp and scornful; then the other, hushed and slow. I saw Godwin lift his finger and point it at the door. I went out, and said to the woman, 'Dr. Godwin wishes to see you; please control yourself.'

"We went back into the room. The wife followed. But Godwin had lost consciousness again. They sat down, those two, and hid their faces. I can see them now, one on each side of the bed, their eyes covered with their hands, each with her claim on him, all murdered by the other's presence; each with her torn love. H'm! What they must have suffered, then! And all the time the child crying—the child of one of them, that might have been the other's!"

The doctor was silent, and the old Director turned towards him his white-bearded, ruddy face, with a look as if he were groping in the dark.

"Just then, I remember," the doctor went on suddenly, "the bells of St. Jude's close by began to peal out for the finish of a wedding. That brought Godwin back to life. He just looked from one woman to the other with a queer, miserable sort of smile, enough to make your heart break. And they both looked at him. The face of the wife—poor thing!—was as bitter hard as a cut stone, but she sat there, without ever stirring a finger. As for the other woman—I couldn't look at her. He beckoned to me; but I couldn't catch his words, the bells drowned them. A minute later he was dead.

"Life's a funny thing! You wake in the morning with your foot firm on the ladder—One touch, and down you go! You snuff out like a candle. And it's lucky when your flame goes out, if only one woman's flame goes out too.

"Neither of those women cried. The wife stayed there by the bed. I got the other one away to her carriage, down the street.—And so she was there to-day! That explains, I think, the look you saw."

The doctor ceased, and in the silence the old Director nodded. Yes! That explained the look he had seen on the face of that unknown woman, the deep, unseizable, weird look. That explained the look he had seen on the wife's face at the funeral twenty years ago!

And peering wistfully, he said:

"They looked—they looked—almost triumphant!"

Then, slowly, he rubbed his hands over his knees, with the secret craving of the old for warmth.

CHAPTER VI

FAIRYLAND

It was about three o'clock, this November afternoon, when I rode down into "Fairyland," as it is called about here. The birch-trees there are more beautiful than any in the world; and when the clouds are streaming over in rain-grey, and the sky soaring above in higher blue, just-seen, those gold and silver creatures have such magical loveliness as makes the hearts of mortals ache. The fairies, who have been driven off the moor, alone watch them with equanimity, if they be not indeed the birch-trees themselves—especially those little very golden ones which have strayed out into the heather, on the far side of the glen. "Revenge!" the fairies cried when a century ago those, whom they do not exist just to amuse, made the new road over the moor, cutting right through the home of twilight, that wood above the "Falls," where till then they had always enjoyed inviolable enchantment. They trooped forthwith in their multitudinous secrecy down into the glen, to swarm about the old road. In half a century or so they had it almost abandoned, save for occasional horsemen and harmless persons seeking beauty, for whom the fairies have never had much feeling of aversion. And now, after a hundred years, it is all theirs; the ground so golden with leaves and bracken that the old track is nothing but a vague hardness beneath a horse's feet, nothing but a runnel for the rains to gather in. There is everywhere that glen scent of mouldering leaves, so sweet when the wind comes down and stirs it, and the sun frees and livens it. Not very many birds, perhaps because hawks are fond of hovering here. This was once the only road up to the village, the only communication with all that lies to the south and east! Now the fairies have got it indeed, they have witched to skeletons all the little bridges across the glen stream; they have mossed and thinned the gates to wraiths. With their dapple-gold revelry in sunlight, and their dance of pied beauty under the moon, they have made all their own.

I have ridden many times down into this glen; and slowly up among the beeches and oaks into the lanes again, hoping and believing that, some day, I should see a fairy take shape to my thick mortal vision; and to-day, at last, I have seen.

I heard it first about half-way up the wood, a silvery voice piping out very true what seemed like mortal words, not quite to be caught. Resolved not to miss it this time, I got off quietly and tied my mare to a tree. Then, tiptoeing in the damp leaves which did not rustle, I stole up till I caught sight of it, from behind an oak.

It was sitting in yellow bracken as high as its head, under a birch-tree that had a few branches still gold-feathered. It seemed to be clothed in blue, and to be swaying as it sang. There was something in its arms, as it might be a creature being nursed. Cautiously I slipped from that tree to the next, till I could see its face, just like a child's, fascinating, very, very delicate, the little open mouth poised and shaped ever so neatly to the words it was singing; the eyes wide apart and ever so wide open, fixed on nothing mortal. The song, and the little body, and the spirit in the eyes, all seemed to sway—sway together, like a soft wind that goes sough-sough, swinging, in the tops of the ferns. And now it stretched out one arm, and now the other, beckoning in to it those to which it was singing; so that one seemed to feel the invisible ones stealing up closer and closer.

These were the words which came so silvery and slow through that little mouth: "Chil-dren, chil-dren! Hussh!"

It seemed as if the very rabbits must come and sit-up there, the jays and pigeons settle above; everything in all the wood gather. Even one's own heart seemed to be drawn in by those beckoning arms, and the slow enchantment of that tinkling voice, and the look in those eyes, which, lost in the unknown, were seeing no mortal glen, but only that mazed wood, where friendly wild things come, who have no sound to their padding, no whirr to the movement of their wings; whose gay whisperings have no noise, whose eager shapes no colour—the fairy dream-wood of the unimaginable.

"Chil-dren, chil-dren! Hus-s-h!"

For just a moment I could see that spirit company, ghosts of the ferns and leaves, of butterflies and bees and birds, and four-footed things innumerable, ghosts of the wind, the sun-beams, and the rain-drops, and tiny flickering ghosts of moon-rays. For just a moment I saw what the fairy's eyes were seeing, without knowing what they saw.

And then my mare trod on a dead branch, and all vanished. My fairy was gone; and there was only little "Connemara," as we called her, nursing her doll, and smiling up at me from the fern, where she had come to practise her new school-song.

CHAPTER VII

THE NIGHTMARE CHILD

I set down here not precisely the words of my friend, the country doctor, but the spirit of them:

"You know there are certain creatures in this world whom one simply dare not take notice of, however sorry one may be for them. That has often been borne in on me. I realised it, I think, before I met that little girl. I used to attend her mother for varicose veins—one of those women who really ought not to have children, since they haven't the very least notion of how to bring them up. The wife of a Sussex agricultural labourer called Alliner, she was a stout person, with most peculiar prominent epileptic eyes, such eyes as one usually associates with men of letters or criminals. And yet there was nothing in her. She was just a lazy, slatternly, easy-going body, rather given to drink. Her husband was a thin, dirty, light-hearted fellow, who did his work and offended nobody. Her eldest daughter, a pretty and capable girl, was wild, got into various kinds of trouble, and had to migrate, leaving two illegitimate children behind her with their grandparents. The younger girl, the child of this story, who was called Emmeline, of all names—pronounced Em'leen, of course—was just fifteen at the time of my visits to her mother. She had eyes like a hare's, a mouth which readily fell open, and brown locks caught back from her scared and knobby forehead. She was thin, and walked with her head poked a little forward, and she so manoeuvred her legs and long feet, of which one turned in rather and seemed trying to get in front of the other, that there was something clodhopperish in her gait. Once in a way you would see her in curl-papers, and then indeed she was plain, poor child! She seemed to have grown up without ever having had the least attention paid to her. I don't think she was ill-treated—she was simply not treated at all. At school they had been kind enough, but had regarded her as almost deficient. Seeing that her father was paid about fifteen shillings a week, that her mother had no conception of housekeeping, and that there were two babies to be fed, they were, of course, villainously poor, and Em'leen was always draggle-tailed and badly shod. One side of her too-short dress seemed ever to hang lower than the other, her stockings always had one hole at least, and her hat—such queer hats—would seem about to fly away. I have known her type in the upper classes pass muster as "eccentric" or "full of character." And even in Em'leen there was a sort of smothered natural comeliness, trying pathetically to push through, and never getting a chance. She always had a lost-dog air, and when her big hare's eyes clung on your face, it seemed as if she only wanted a sign to make her come trailing at your heels, looking up for a pat or a bit of biscuit.

"She went to work, of course, the moment she left school. Her first place was in a small farm where they took lodgers, and her duties were to do everything, without, of course, knowing how to do anything. She had to leave because she used to take soap and hairpins, and food that was left over, and was once seen licking a dish. It was just about then that I attended her mother for those veins in her unwieldy legs, and the child was at home, waiting to secure some other fate. It was impossible not to look at that little creature kindly, and to speak to her now and then; she would not exactly light up, because her face was not made that way, but she would hang towards you as if you were a magnet, and you had at once the uncomfortable sensation that you might find her clinging, impossible to shake off. If one passed her in the village, too, or coming down from her blackberrying in the thickets on the Downs—their cottage lay just below the South Downs—one knew that she would be lingering along, looking back till you were out of sight. Somehow one hardly thought of her as a girl at all, she seemed so far from all human hearts, so wandering in a queer lost world of her own, and to imagine what she could be thinking was as impossible as it is with animals. Once I passed her and her mother dawdling slowly in a lane, then heard the dot-and-go-one footsteps pattering after me, and the childish voice, rather soft and timid, say behind my shoulder: "Would you please buy some blackberries, sir?" She was almost pretty at that moment, flushed and breathless at having actually spoken to me, but her eyes hanging on my face brought a sort of nightmare feeling at once of being unable to get rid of her.

"Isn't it a cruel thing when you come to think of it, that there should be born into the world poor creatures—children, dogs, cats, horses—who want badly to love and be loved, and yet whom no one can quite put up with, much less feel affection for!

"Well, what happened to her is what will always happen to such as those, one way or another, in a world where the callous abound; for, however unlovable a woman or girl, she has her use to a man, just as a dog or a horse has to a master who cares nothing for it.

"Soon after I bought those blackberries I went out to France on military duty. I got my leave a year later, and went home. It was late September, very lovely weather, and I took a real holiday walking or lying about up on the Downs, and only coming down at sunset. On one of those days when you really enter heaven, so pure are the lines of the hills, so cool the blue, the green, the chalk-white colouring under the smile of the afternoon sun—I was returning down that same lane, when I came on Em'leen sitting in a gap of the bank, with her dishevelled hat beside her, and her chin sunk on her hands. My appearance seemed to drag her out of a heavy dream—her eyes awoke, became startled, rolled furtively; she scrambled up, dropped her little, old school curtsey, then all confused, faced the bank as if she were going to climb it. She was taller, her dress longer, her hair gathered up, and it was very clear what was soon going to happen to her. I walked on in a rage. At her age—barely sixteen even yet! I am a doctor, and accustomed to most things, but this particular crime against children of that helpless sort does make my blood boil. Nothing, not even passion to excuse it—who could feel passion for that poor child?—nothing but the cold, clumsy lust of some young ruffian. Yes, I walked on in a rage, and went straight to her mother's cottage. That wretched woman was incapable of moral indignation, or else the adventures of her elder daughter had exhausted her powers of expression. 'Yes,' she admitted, 'Em'leen had got herself into trouble too, but she would not tell, she wouldn't say nothin' against nobody. It was a bad business, surely, an' now there would be three o' them, an' Alliner was properly upset, that he was!' That was all there was to be had out of her. One felt that she knew or suspected more, but her fingers had been so burned over the elder girl that anything to her was better than a fuss.

"I saw Alliner; he was a decent fellow, though dirty, distressed in his simple, shallow-pated way, and more obviously ignorant than his wife. I spoke to the schoolmistress, a shrewd and kindly married woman.

"Poor Emmeline! Yes, she had noticed. It was very sad and wicked! She hinted, but would not do more than hint, at the son of the miller, but he was back again, fighting in France now, and, after all, her evidence amounted to no more than his reputation with girls. Besides, one is very careful what one says in a country village. I, however, was so angry that I should not have been careful if I could have got hold of anything at all definite.

"I did not see the child again before my leave was up. The very next thing I heard of her, was in a newspaper—Emmeline Alliner, sixteen, had been committed for trial for causing the death of her illegitimate child by exposure. I was on the sick list in January, and went home to rest. I had not been there two days before I received a visit from a solicitor of our assize town, who came to ask me if I would give evidence at the girl's trial as to the nature of her home surroundings. I learned from him the details of the lugubrious business. It seems that she had slipped out one bitter afternoon in December, barely a fortnight after her confinement, carrying her baby. There was snow on the ground, and it was freezing hard, but the sun was bright, and it was that perhaps which tempted her. She must have gone up towards the Downs by the lane where I had twice met her; gone up, and stopped at the very gap in the bank where she had been sitting lost in that heavy dream when I saw her last. She appears to have subsided there in the snow, for there she was found by the postman just as it was getting dark, leaning over her knees as if stupefied, with her chin buried in her hands—and the baby stiff and dead in the snow beside her. When I told the lawyer how I had seen her there ten weeks before, and of the curious dazed state she had been in, he said at once: 'Ah! the exact spot. That's very important; it looks uncommonly as if it were there that she came by her misfortune. What do you think? It's almost evident that she'd lost sense of her surroundings, baby and all. I shall ask you to tell us about that at the trial. She's a most peculiar child; I can't get anything out of her. I keep asking her for the name of the man, or some indication of how it came about, but all she says is: "Nobody—nobody!" Another case of immaculate conception! Poor little creature, she's very pathetic, and that's her best chance. Who could condemn a child like that?'

"And so indeed it turned out. I spared no feelings in my evidence. The mother and father were in court, and I hope Mrs. Alliner liked my diagnosis of her maternal qualities. My description of how Em'leen was sitting when I met her in September tallied so exactly with the postman's account of how he met her, that I could see the jury were impressed. And then there was the figure of the child herself, lonely there in the dock. The French have a word, Hébétée. Surely there never was a human object to which it applied better. She stood like a little tired pony, whose head hangs down, half-sleeping after exertion; and those hare eyes of hers were glued to the judge's face, for all the world as if she were worshipping him. It must have made him extraordinarily uncomfortable. He summed up very humanely, dwelling on the necessity of finding intention in her conduct towards the baby; and he used some good strong language against the unknown man. The jury found her not guilty, and she was discharged. The schoolmistress and I, anticipating this, had found her a refuge with some Sisters of Mercy, who ran a sort of home not far away, and to that we took her, without a 'by your leave' to the mother.

"When I came home the following summer, I found an opportunity of going to look her up. She was amazingly improved in face and dress, but she had attached herself to one of the Sisters—a broad, fine-looking woman—to such a pitch that she seemed hardly alive when out of her sight. The Sister spoke of it to me with real concern.

"'I really don't know what to do with her,' she said; 'she seems incapable of anything unless I tell her; she only feels things through me. It's really quite trying, and sometimes very funny, poor little soul! but it's tragic for her. If I told her to jump out of her bedroom window, or lie down in that pond and drown, she'd do it without a moment's hesitation. She can't go through life like this; she must learn to stand on her own feet. We must try and get her a good place, where she can learn what responsibility means, and get a will of her own.'

"I looked at the Sister, so broad, so capable, so handsome, and so puzzled, and I thought, 'Yes, I know exactly. She's on your nerves; and where in the world will you find a place for her where she won't become a sort of nightmare to some one, with her devotion, or else get it taken advantage of again?' And I urged them to keep her a little longer. They did; for when I went home for good, six months later, I found that she had only just gone into a place with an old lady-patient of mine, in a small villa on the outskirts of our village. She used to open the door to me when I called there on my rounds once a week. She retained vestiges of the neatness which had been grafted on her by the Sister, but her frock was already beginning to sag down on one side, and her hair to look ill-treated. The old lady spoke to her with a sort of indulgent impatience, and it was clear that the girl's devotion was not concentrated upon her. I caught myself wondering what would be its next object, never able to help the feeling that if I gave a sign it would be myself. You may be sure I gave no sign. What's the good? I hold the belief that people should not force themselves to human contacts or relationships which they cannot naturally and without irritation preserve. I've seen these heroic attempts come to grief so often; in fact, I don't think I've ever seen one succeed, not even between blood relations. In the long run they merely pervert and spoil the fibre of the attempter, without really benefiting the attemptee. Behind healthy relationships between human beings, or even between human beings and animals, there must be at least some rudimentary affinity. That's the tragedy of poor little souls like Em'leen. Where on earth can they find the affinity which makes life good? The very fact that they must worship is their destruction. It was a soldier—or so they said—who had brought her to her first grief; I had seen her adoring the judge at the trial, then the handsome uniformed Sister. And I, as the village doctor, was a sort of tin-pot deity in those parts, so I was very careful to keep my manner to her robust and almost brusque.

"And then one day I passed her coming from the post office; she was looking back, her cheeks were flushed, and she was almost pretty. There by the inn a butcher's cart was drawn up. The young butcher, new to our village (he had a stiff knee, and had been discharged from the Army), was taking out a leg of mutton. He had a daredevil face; and eyes that had seen much death. He had evidently been chatting with her, for he was still smiling, and even as I passed him he threw her a jerk of the head.

"Two Sundays after that I was coming down past Wiley's copse at dusk, and heard a man's coarse laugh. There, through a tiny gap in the nut-bushes, I saw a couple seated. He had his leg stiffly stretched out, and his arm round the girl, who was leaning towards him; her lips were parted, and those hare's eyes of hers were looking up into his face. Adoration!

"I don't know what it was my duty to have done, I only know that I did nothing, but slunk on with a lump in my throat.

"Adoration! There it was again! Hopeless! Incurable devotions to those who cared no more for her than for a slice of suet-pudding to be eaten hot, gulped down, forgotten, or loathed in the recollection. And there they are, these girls, one to almost every village of this country—a nightmare to us all. The look on her face was with me all that evening and in my dreams.

"I know no more, for two days later I was summoned North to take up work in a military hospital."

CHAPTER VIII

BUTTERCUP-NIGHT

Why is it that in some places one has such a feeling of life being, not merely a long picture-show for human eyes, but a single breathing, glowing, growing thing, of which we are no more important a part than the swallows and magpies, the foals and sheep in the meadows, the sycamores and ash-trees and flowers in the fields, the rocks and little bright streams, or even than the long fleecy clouds and their soft-shouting drivers, the winds?

True, we register these parts of being, and they—so far as we know—do not register us; yet it is impossible to feel, in such places as I speak of, the busy, dry, complacent sense of being all that matters, which in general we humans have so strongly.

In these rare spots, which are always in the remote country, untouched by the advantages of civilisation, one is conscious of an enwrapping web or mist of spirit—is it, perhaps the glamourous and wistful wraith of all the vanished shapes once dwelling there in such close comradeship?

It was Sunday of an early June when I first came on one such, far down in the West country. I had walked with my knapsack twenty miles; and, there being no room at the tiny inn of the very little village, they directed me to a wicket gate, through which, by a path leading down a field, I would come to a farm-house, where I might find lodging. The moment I got into that field I felt within me a peculiar contentment, and sat down on a rock to let the feeling grow. In an old holly-tree rooted to the bank about fifty yards away, two magpies evidently had a nest, for they were coming and going, avoiding my view as much as possible, yet with a certain stealthy confidence which made one feel that they had long prescriptive right to that dwelling-place. Around, far as one could see, was hardly a yard of level ground; all hill and hollow, long ago reclaimed from the moor; and against the distant folds of the hills the farm-house and its thatched barns were just visible, embowered amongst beeches and some dark trees, with a soft bright crown of sunlight over the whole. A gentle wind brought a faint rustling up from those beeches, and from a large lime-tree which stood by itself; on this wind some little snowy clouds, very high and fugitive in that blue heaven, were always moving over. But I was most struck by the buttercups. Never was field so lighted up by those tiny lamps, those little bright pieces of flower china out of the Great Pottery. They covered the whole ground, as if the sunlight had fallen bodily from the sky, in millions of gold patines; and the fields below as well, down to what was evidently a stream, were just as thick with the extraordinary warmth and glory of them.

Leaving the rock at last, I went towards the house. It was long and low, and rather sad, standing in a garden all mossy grass and buttercups, with a few rhododendrons and flowery shrubs, below a row of fine old Irish yews. On the stone verandah a grey sheep-dog and a very small golden-haired child were sitting close together, absorbed in each other. A woman came in answer to my knock, and told me, in a pleasant soft, slurring voice, that I might stay the night; and dropping my knapsack, I went out again. Through an old gate under a stone arch I came on the farmyard, quite deserted save for a couple of ducks moving slowly down a gutter in the sunlight; and noticing the upper half of a stable-door open, I went across, in search of something living. There, in a rough loose-box, on thick straw, lay a chestnut, long-tailed mare, with the skin and head of a thoroughbred. She was swathed in blankets, and her face, all cut about the cheeks and over the eyes, rested on an ordinary human's pillow, held by a bearded man in shirt-sleeves; while, leaning against the white-washed walls, sat fully a dozen other men, perfectly silent, very gravely and intently gazing. The mare's eyes were half-closed, and what could be seen of them was dull and blueish, as though she had been through a long time of pain. Save for her rapid breathing, she lay quite still, but her neck and ears were streaked with sweat, and every now and then her hind-legs quivered. Seeing me at the door, she raised her head, uttering a queer, half-human noise; but the bearded man at once put his hand on her forehead, and with a "Woa, my dear, woa, my pretty!" pressed it down again, while with the other hand he plumped up the pillow for her cheek. And, as the mare obediently let fall her head, one of the men said in a low voice: "I never see anything so like a Christian!" and the others echoed him, in chorus, "Like a Christian—like a Christian!" It went to one's heart to watch her, and I moved off down the farm lane into an old orchard, where the apple-trees were still in bloom, with bees—very small ones—busy on the blossoms, whose petals were dropping on to the dock leaves and buttercups in the long grass. Climbing over the bank at the far end, I found myself in a meadow the like of which—so wild and yet so lush—I think I have never seen. Along one hedge of its meandering length were masses of pink mayflower; and between two little running streams quantities of yellow water iris—"daggers," as they call them—were growing; the "print-frock" orchis, too, was all over the grass, and everywhere the buttercups. Great stones coated with yellowish moss were strewn among the ash-trees and dark hollies; and through a grove of beeches on the far side, such as Corot might have painted, a girl was running with a youth after her, who jumped down over the bank and vanished. Thrushes, blackbirds, yaffles, cuckoos, and one other very monotonous little bird were in full song; and this, with the sound of the streams, and the wind, and the shapes of the rocks and trees, the colours of the flowers, and the warmth of the sun, gave one a feeling of being lost in a very wilderness of Nature. Some ponies came slowly from the far end, tangled, gipsy-headed little creatures, stared, and went off again at speed. It was just one of those places where any day the Spirit of all Nature might start up in one of those white gaps which separate the trees and rocks. But though I sat a long time waiting, hoping—Pan did not come.

They were all gone from the stable, when I went back to the farm, except the bearded nurse, and one tall fellow, who might have been the "Dying Gaul," as he crouched there in the straw; and the mare was sleeping—her head between her nurse's knees.

That night I woke at two o'clock, to find it bright as day, almost, with moonlight coming in through the flimsy curtains. And, smitten with the feeling which comes to us creatures of routine so rarely—of what beauty and strangeness we let slip by without ever stretching out hand to grasp it—I got up, dressed, stole downstairs, and out.

Never was such a night of frozen beauty, never such dream-tranquillity. The wind had dropped, and the silence was such that one hardly liked to tread even on the grass. From the lawn and fields there seemed to be a mist rising—in truth, the moonlight caught on the dewy buttercups; and across this ghostly radiance the shadows of the yew-trees fell in dense black bars. Suddenly, I bethought me of the mare. How was she faring, this marvellous night? Very softly opening the door into the yard, I tiptoed across. A light was burning in her box. And I could hear her making the same half-human noise she had made in the afternoon, as if wondering at her feelings; and instantly the voice of the bearded man talking to her as one might talk to a child: "Oover, me darlin'; yu've a-been long enough o' that side. Wa-ay, my swate—yu let old Jack turn 'u, then!" Then came a scuffling in the straw, a thud, again that half-human sigh, and his voice: "Putt your 'ead to piller, that's my dandy gel. Old Jack wouldn' 'urt 'u; no more'n ef 'u was the queen!" Then only her quick breathing could be heard, and his cough and mutter, as he settled down once more to his long vigil. I crept very softly up to the window, but she heard me at once; and at the movement of her head the old fellow sat up, blinking his eyes out of the bush of his grizzled hair and beard. Opening the door, I said:

"May I come in?"

"Oo, ay! Come in, Zurr, if 'u'm a mind to."

I sat down beside him on a sack, and for some time we did not speak, taking each other in. One of his legs was lame, so that he had to keep it stretched out all the time; and awfully tired he looked, grey-tired.

"You're a great nurse!" I said at last. "It must be hard work, watching out here all night."

His eyes twinkled; they were of that bright grey kind through which the soul looks out.

"Aw, no!" he said. "Ah don't grudge it vur a dumb animal. Poor things—they can't 'elp theirzelves. Many's the naight ah've zat up with 'orses and beasts tu. 'Tes en me—can't bear to zee dumb creatures zuffer!" And, laying his hand on the mare's ears: "They zay 'orses 'aven't no souls. 'Tes my belief they'm gotten souls, zame as us. Many's the Christian ah've seen ain't got the soul of an 'orse. Zame with the beasts—an' the sheep; 'tes only they can't spake their minds."

"And where," I said, "do you think they go to when they die?" He looked at me a little queerly, fancying, perhaps, that I was leading him into some trap; making sure, too, that I was a real stranger, without power over him, body or soul—for humble folk in the country must be careful; then, reassured, and nodding in his bushy beard, he answered knowingly:

"Ah don't think they goes zo very far!"

"Why? Do you ever see their spirits?"

"Naw, naw; I never zeen none; but, for all they zay, ah don't think none of us goes such a brave way off. There's room for all, dead or alive. An' there's Christians ah've zeen—well, ef they'm not dead for gude, then neither aren't dumb animals, for sure."

"And rabbits, squirrels, birds, even insects? How about them?"

He was silent, as if I had carried him a little beyond the confines of his philosophy, then shook his head:

"'Tes all a bit dimsy-like. But yu watch dumb animals, Zurr, even the laste littlest one, and yu'll zee they knows a lot more'n what us thenks; an' they du's things, tu, that putts shame on a man's often as not. They've a got that in 'em as passes show." And not noticing my stare at that unconscious plagiarism, he added: "Ah'd zuuner zet up of a naight with an 'orse than with an 'uman; they've more zense, and patience." And, stroking the mare's forehead, he added: "Now, my dear, time for yu t' 'ave yure bottle."

I waited to see her take her draught, and lay her head down once more on the pillow. Then, hoping he would get a sleep, I rose to go.

"Aw, 'tes nothin' much," he said, "this time o' year; not like in winter. 'Twill come day before yu know, these buttercup-nights"; and twinkling up at me out of his kindly bearded face, he settled himself again into the straw. I stole a look back at his rough figure propped against the sack, with the mare's head down beside his knee, at her swathed chestnut body, and the gold of the straw, the white walls, and dusky nooks and shadows of that old stable, illumined by the "dimsy" light of the old lantern. And with the sense of having seen something holy, I crept away up into the field where I had lingered the day before, and sat down on the same half-way rock. Close on dawn it was, the moon still sailing wide over the moor, and the flowers of this "buttercup-night" fast closed, not taken in at all by her cold glory!

Most silent hour of all the twenty-four—when the soul slips half out of sheath, and hovers in the cool; when the spirit is most in tune with what, soon or late, happens to all spirits; hour when a man cares least whether or no he be alive, as we understand the word.... "None of us goes such a brave way off—there's room for all, dead or alive." Though it was almost unbearably colourless, and quiet, there was warmth in thinking of those words of his; in the thought, too, of the millions of living things snugly asleep all round; warmth in realising that unanimity of sleep. Insects and flowers, birds, men, beasts, the very leaves on the trees—away in slumber-land. Waiting for the first bird to chirrup, one had, perhaps, even a stronger feeling than in daytime of the unity and communion of all life, of the subtle brotherhood of living things that fall all together into oblivion, and, all together, wake.

When dawn comes, while moonlight is still powdering the world's face, quite a long time passes before one realises how the quality of the light has changed; and so, it was day before I knew it. Then the sun came up above the hills; dew began to sparkle, and colour to stain the sky. That first praise of the sun from every bird and leaf and blade of grass, the tremulous flush and chime of dawn! One has strayed far from the heart of things that it should come as something strange and wonderful! Indeed, I noticed that the beasts and birds gazed at me as if I simply could not be there at this hour which so belonged to them. And to me, too, they seemed strange and new—with that in them "which passeth show," and as of a world where man did not exist, or existed only as just another sort of beast or bird.

But just then began the crowning glory of that dawn—the opening and lighting of the buttercups. Not one did I actually see unclose, yet, of a sudden, they were awake, and the fields once more a blaze of gold.

John Galsworthy – A Short Biography

John Galsworthy, eldest son of John Galsworthy (1817-1904), a solicitor and company director of Old Jewry, London, and Blanche Bailey (1835-1915), daughter of Charles Bartleet, a needlemaker in Redditch. His father's ancestors originated in Wembury, near Plymouth in England, and Galsworthy, for whom family origins were of significant importance, maintained a close connection with Devon. His more immediate family were considerably wealthy and well established in the shipping industry, and owned a fine estate in Kingston-upon-Thames called Parkfield, where Galsworthy was born on the 14th August 1867. At the age of nine he began education at Saugeen, a Bournemouth preparatory school, before starting at Harrow school in 1881 where he remained until 1886, distinguishing himself as an athlete.

His education at Harrow being successful enough to gain him entrance to Oxford, he began at New College to read law and gained a second-class degree with honours in 1889. Following Lincoln's Inn he was called to the bar in 1890. Despite this recognition he realised that he was not keen to actually begin practising law and so he resolved instead to look after the family's shipping business while specialising himself in Marine Law. This decision saw him take to the seas to destinations such as Vancouver, Island and South AFrica, though it was at the age of twenty-five on one particular journey to Australia, motivated by an (unfulfilled) intention to meet Robert Louis Stevenson on Samoa that he would being to realise fully his literary interests: though he was not considering becoming a writer at this time, his enjoyment of literature was enough to encourage an attempt at meeting a great writer and eventually enabled one of the most significant encounters of his life. He made the journey with his friend Edward Sanderson and, though he missed Stevenson, he met Joseph Conrad, a fellow future author famed for his novels which were often nautically themed. At the time Conrad was the first mate of the sailing-ship Torrens moored in the harbour of Adelaide, Australia; still very much focused on his ship-borne career, he was yet to begin his writing in earnest.

Indeed, though neither knew at the time, both Conrad and Galsworthy were at similar junctures in their lives, their time spent as sea acting as a transitional period during which each found their literary calling. It is perhaps owning to this unknown common ground that they became close friends. During his time on the Torrens Galsworthy recorded several details, offering a frank and valuable characterisation of Conrad while also illuminating his own experiences as a student of Marine Law.

"I supposed to be studying navigation for the Admiralty Bar, would every day work out the position of the ship with the captain. On one side of the saloon table we would sit and check our observations with those of Conrad, who from the other side of the table would look at us a little quizzically."

On his return to England and the cessation of his nautical voyaging, Galsworthy began an affair with the wife of his first cousin, Major Arthur John Galsworthy. Ada Nemesis Pearson Cooper (1864-1956), the daughter of Emanuel Copper, an obstetrician from Norwich, remained married to the Major for ten years and the affair remained secret for its duration. In order to conceal the affair they took considerable pains to avoid suspicion. One such tactic was to stay in a secluded farmhouse called Wingstone in the village on Manaton on Dartmoor, in Devon. In Galsworthy's decision to choose Devon as the location for their clandestine rendezvous we see evidence of Galsworthy's affection for the place of his father's origin. It was only when, in 1905, she divorced the Major that their affair became known following their marriage on 23rd September of that year.

Galsworthy now took to writing sometime after having met Conrad and his career began in earnest when, in 1897, his first work, From the Four Winds, a volume of short stories, was published under the pseudonym John Sinjohn. He succeeded this in 1898 with Jocelyn, his first novel, and then his second in 1900, Villa Rubein. In 1901 he published a second volume of short stories, A Man of Devon, which was the last of his work to be published under pseudonym. The first of his work to be published under his own name was The Island Pharisees in 1904, a novel of social observation, seasoned with flashes of satire and propaganda. His decision to write under his own name is arguably owing to the recent death of his father, either as a mark of respect to his name or because now he was able to publish freely without incurring the possibility of paternal disappointment at his choice of career. It also marked a shift in his professionalism; he had hitherto published with small, independent publishers, but The Island Pharisees was published by Heinemann, a far more established House and one with whom he remained for the duration of his writing career.

He arguably cemented his position and maturity as a writer when, in 1906, he saw the publication of both his first major play, The Silver Box, and the novel The Man of Property. Each was published to considerable critical acclaim, and to achieve both in such a short space of time was impressive. the Silver Box concerns the imbalance in the justice system with regards to criminals of differing class by contrasting the treatment of a poor thief and a rich thief, both of whom stole silver cigarette cases but for very different reasons. The complexity of individual experience when not dealt with in public is highlighted and questioned in a bravely critical manner; despite the clear issues it raises with class and privilege, the final night was attended by the Price and Princess of Wales. The Man of Property was the first novel in the famous The Forsyte Saga, a trilogy of novels with an 'interlude' between each one, written between 1906 and 1921. Dealing with the questions of status, class and materialism, The Man of Property introduces us to the Forsyte family, particularly Soames Forsyte, who is acutely aware of his status as 'new money' and equally keen to assert himself as a wealthy man. Jealous of his wife and desperate to own things in order to confirm his wealth to those observing him, he engineers a plan to keep his wife from her friends which backfires spectacularly when, instead of cutting her off, all Soames achieves is enabling her to have an affair. This drives Soames to terrible actions with terrible consequences, which Galsworthy depicts with confidence.

Very typically Edwardian, the novel focuses on conflict between property and art, and to a certain degree much of its emotional power is drawn from Galsworthy's own life, particularly his affair with Ada. Their rendezvous in the countryside of Devon mirror the manner in which Forsyte seeks to relocate his wife and; though theirs was a much healthier relationship, there are clear similarities. By examining the fragile nature of the class system and those moving within it Galsworthy offered an important perspective on the relationships between material wealth, personal happiness and obsession, and the manner in which these change over time. His contemporaries widely regarded the publication of this novel as marking the end of Victorianism. His friend Conrad praised it as "indubitably a piece of art" and, though the notoriously risqué D.H. Lawrence lamented the novel's timidity in the face of sexuality and sensuality, he considered it potentially "a very great novel, a very great satire".

Though he continued to write both plays and novels, it was his work as a playwright for which he was most celebrated by his contemporaries. Indeed, his next novel, The Country House, seems uncharacteristically unfocused, its satirical view of those belonging to the country set comparatively unremarkable and weakly characterised, while at times the tone of satire becomes one of ironic detachment. In 1909 he published Fraternity, an exploration of of the various connections between urban society and the social classes therein, though its representation of lower-class Londoners is utterly unconvincing and ill-informed. Remaining with the subject of the landed gentry and the society surrounding it, in 1915 he published The Freelands, which does not stray far from conservative discussions of capitalism, the rural economy and their interrelationship.

His drama, however, featured a convincingly muted realism, directed at a relatively small, educated and politically-aware audience. His social agenda is prevalent here too, and is represented in a simple and static manner producing arresting instances of high drama. This talent for creating moments of captivating theatre is complimented by an instinctual sense of balance enabling his narratives to vacillate between their emotional high- and low-points, ultimately reaching conclusive equilibrium. This is particularly evident in one of his most popular plays, Strife, published in 1909 and examining the antagonists in a strike at a Cornish tin mine. In this, and in 1910's Justice, he approaches his subject with sympathy, irony and balance, which establishes a position of narrative authority while garnering the audiences trust that he is representing his characters and their motives justly. Justice condemns the use of solitary confinement in prisons, a reformist agenda which caught the liberality of his contemporary audiences along with the home secretary, Winston Churchill. Despite he was careful to disassociate himself with politics and professed himself apolitical, he and his work were nevertheless aligned with the views of the Liberal establishment. He spent much of the duration of the First World War working in a field hospital in France as an orderly having been passed over for military service.

Despite the popularity and brilliance of his work, it was only in 1920 that he had his first true commercial success with The Skin Game, a melodrama dealing with ethics, property and class. The play was adapted by Alfred Hitchcock in 1931. Galsworthy, meanwhile, had turned down a knighthood in 1918, considering his work not sufficient to be made a knight of the realm. He did, however, accept the Belgian Palmes d'Or in the following year. In 1920 he published the second novel in the Forsyte Saga, In Chancery, in which he resumes many of the themes of the first novel, focusing on the marital disharmony between Soames Forsyte and his wife. Katherine Mansfield considered it "a fascinating, brilliant book" in her review in The Atheneum. Then, in 1921, he was elected as the PEN International Literary Club's first president. The concluding novel to The Forsyte Saga, To Let was published in 1921 with a kind of peace being found between Forsyte and his now-ex wife, though he is left contemplating his losses and his greed. More ironic treatment of class confusions followed in Loyalties, bringing with it more popular success which lasted until 1926 and Escape, the last of his popular plays. Though he enjoyed popular success it was inconsistent and relatively small. His Collected Plays was published in 1929.

Over the course of time the appreciation of his work has gradually shifted from his plays to his novels, and particularly the detail and intricacy of his chronicle of English social difference, tension and pretension in The Forsyte Saga. Its success encouraged Galsworthy to revisit Soames Forsyte in a second trilogy, A Modern Comedy, which follows Soames's obsessive love of his daughter Fleur. In its three volumes, The White Monkey (1924), The Silver Spoon (1936) and Swan Song (1928) he examines the

English commercial upper-middle class and its ideologies, its instinct to possess as its only way of distinguishing itself manifested in the poisonous materialism of Soames. Interestingly, this emergent social class which he so vehemently criticises is the very class from which he emerged. He witnessed first-hand its insularity, its chauvinism, its restrictive and oppressive morality, its stubborn imperialism and its materialism, and it is this experience which enables him to write so comfortably about it. Swan Song is widely considered among the best of Galsworthy's writing for the depth of its exploration of society and its heightened emotional subtlety. In 1929 he was appointed to the Order of Merit, despite having turned down a knighthood earlier. He spent his last years writing a third trilogy, End of the Chapter, beginning in 1931 with Maid in Waiting, Flowering Wilderness in 1932 and concluding with Over The River in 1933. These are significantly less coherent works and are indicative of his deteriorating health. Indeed, in 1932 he was awarded the Nobel Prize, though he was too ill to attend the ceremony.

Throughout the course of his career he received honorary degrees from the universities of St Andrews (1922), Manchester (1927), Dublin (1929), Cambridge (1930), Sheffield (1930), Oxford (1931), and Princeton (1931). In 1926 New College, Oxford, elected him as an honourary fellow. In photographs he is portrayed as handsome, fastidiously dressed and dignified. He was unusually compassionate and this saw him involved in several charitable and humane causes throughout the course of his life, including penal reforms, attacks on theatrical censorship and campaigning for animal rights. Though he spent the majority of the final seven years of his life at his home in Bury, West Sussex, it was at his home in Hampstead, London, that he died of a brain tumour on 31st January, 1933, six weeks after having been too ill to attend the ceremony in honour of his receiving the Nobel Prize. According to demands made in his will he was cremated and his ashes scattered over the South Downs from an aeroplane. Also in his will was his wish to leave cottages to several of his astonished tenants. He is memorialised in Highgate 'New' Cemetery and in the cloisters of New College, Oxford, where he was an honourary fellow.

John Galsworthy – A Concise Bibliography

From the Four Winds, 1897 (as John Sinjohn)
Jocelyn, 1898 (as John Sinjohn)
Villa Rubein, 1900 (as John Sinjohn)
A Man of Devon, 1901 (as John Sinjohn)
The Island Pharisees, 1904
The Silver Box, 1906 (his first play)
The Man of Property, 1906 – First book of The Forsyte Saga (1922)
The Country House, 1907
A Commentary, 1908
Fraternity, 1909
A Justification for the Censorship of Plays, 1909
Strife, 1909
Fraternity, 1909
Joy, 1909
Justice, 1910
A Motley, 1910
The Spirit of Punishment, 1910
Horses in Mines, 1910
The Patrician, 1911
The Little Dream, 1911

The Pigeon, 1912
The Eldest Son, 1912
Quality, 1912
Moods, Songs, and Doggerels, 1912
For Love of Beasts, 1912
The Inn of Tranquillity, 1912
The Dark Flower, 1913
The Fugitive, 1913
The Mob, 1914
The Freelands, 1915
The Little Man, 1915
A Bit o' Love, 1915
A Sheaf, 1916
The Apple Tree, 1916
The Foundations, 1917
Beyond, 1917
Five Tales, 1918
Indian Summer of a Forsyte, 1918 – First interlude of The Forsyte Saga
Saint's Progress, 1919
Addresses in America, 1912
In Chancery, 1920 – Second book of The Forsyte Saga
Awakening, 1920 – Second interlude of The Forsyte Saga
The Skin Game, 1920
To Let, 1921 – Third book of The Forsyte Saga
A Family Man, 1922
The Little Man, 1922
Loyalties, 1922
Windows, 1922
Captures, 1923
Abracadabra, 1924
The Forest, 1924
Old English, 1924
The White Monkey, 1924 – First book of A Modern Comedy
The Show, 1925
Escape, 1926
The Silver Spoon, 1926 – Second book of A Modern Comedy
Verses New and Old, 1926
Castles in Spain, 1927
A Silent Wooing, 1927 – First Interlude of A Modern Comedy
Passers By, 1927 – Second Interlude of A Modern Comedy
Swan Song, 1928 – Third book of A Modern Comedy
The Manaton Edition, 1923–26 (collection, 30 vols.)
Exiled, 1929
The Roof, 1929
On Forsyte 'Change, 1930
Two Essays on Conrad, 1930
Soames and the Flag, 1930
The Creation of Character in Literature, 1931 (The Romanes Lecture for 1931).

Maid in Waiting, 1931 – First book of End of the Chapter (1934)
Forty Poems, 1932
Flowering Wilderness, 1932 – Second book of End of the Chapter
Autobiographical Letters of Galsworthy: A Correspondence with Frank Harris, 1933
One More River (originally Over the River), 1933 – Third book of End of the Chapter
The Grove Edition, 1927–34 (collection, 27 Vols.)
Collected Poems, 1934
Punch and Go, 1935
The Life and Letters, 1935
The Winter Garden, 1935
Forsytes, Pendyces and Others, 1935
Selected Short Stories, 1935
Glimpses and Reflections, 1937

www.ingramcontent.com/pod-product-compliance
Lightning Source LLC
Chambersburg PA
CBHW071409170626
46811CB00003B/1321